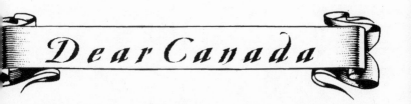

Dear Canada

THESE ARE MY WORDS

The Residential School Diary of Violet Pesheens

BY RUBY SLIPPERJACK

Scholastic Canada Ltd.

Northern Ontario, 1966

Friday, September 9, 1966

They took everything away when I arrived here. I have nothing of the things I had packed in the small suitcase Grandma gave me. I had stones from home and some feathers that Grandma gave me. They took my diary too, the one Grandma gave me for my birthday. It was blue and it even had a shiny gold lock on it, and tiny little keys. I had a lot of stuff written in there that I thought would give me some comfort over the year. But, now it's gone.

I was given this notebook and pencils for school, so I am going to start another diary in this notebook. I am going to hide it with me all the time. I'm writing in very small letters, with the lines close together, because I realize that I can't just write like I normally do if I am going to always hide it.

This is all I remember about what I'd written in my diary yesterday.

We left on the noon train. There were two of us, just me and Emma. Grandma walked with me to the train station. I cried when I hugged her goodbye. She told me to be a good girl and to be strong. She put a hand on my head and over my chest.

At every stop, there were many mothers standing at the station, crying, as more kids got on the train. There were two boys across from me who were laughing and teasing each other, clearly enjoying the trip. When the sun began to set, I was ready to turn around and go back home. That's when I noticed that I had written in my diary that I think this train should be called The Train of Tears. As the afternoon wore on, I wanted to go home already! There were eight of us sitting together now, all going to the same place.

I am getting very hungry. There's a small water fountain by the toilet door. Beside it is a metal thing on the wall that holds small pointy-bottomed paper cups. I pulled one out and poured some water in it, but it tasted funny.

It was getting dark when we got off the train and went to a hotel. We were given two rooms. One was for the boys and one for the girls. We were very hungry but we had no money to go into the dining room. There was a lot of noise from the barroom downstairs. During the night, we could hear fighting downstairs and in the parking lot below. We were very scared. Sometime after midnight, we scrambled up and looked out the window and we saw two men throw a man into the back of a truck and they drove off. There was so much noise and we were too scared to sleep.

Early this morning, we went to the train station and waited for another train that goes south to the city where we are going. We got a brown paper sandwich bag each from the hotel. We were very hungry, and tired from not getting any sleep.

After we settled into our seats on the train, we opened the bags and found a sandwich and an apple in each one.

It was close to lunchtime when we managed to open a window on the coach and stuck our heads out. After several hours, we realized that we had gathered a lot of dirt and soot from the engine onto our hair and faces! We smelled like engine smoke! I got a piece of paper towel from the toilet and wet it in the little sink and wiped my face, and the paper came off black. When you flushed the toilet, it opened a round flap and you could see the train tracks and ties going by below.

We are here at the Residential School now. It is afternoon and I am very tired.

Emma and four of the boys were taken away by a man in a car when we got off the train. Emma said that they'll be living in other people's homes and go to a high school. She said she would come and visit me as often as she could.

There was a man with another car to pick the three of us up at the train station. We drove for a long time before he left the road and turned up a very long drive with tall trees on either side. Then I saw the building. It's a very tall and very, very big brick building and has wide steps going up. It is the biggest building I have ever seen. I got very scared then. I felt so very small. The building loomed above us as we went up the steps and through the door and were told to wait and that we would be called into the office one by one.

When it was my turn, there was a man behind the desk in front of the window and I could not see him clearly with the window behind him. He told me his name and he wrote my name down. Then he told me a list of rules and other stuff that I can't remember. I do remember that I'm never to speak in my own language and that I'll be punished if I do. I am to speak in English only.

When I came out, the boy who arrived with us was gone. The girl was still there, sitting on one of the four chairs beside the door.

Then a woman in a grey skirt and white blouse came and got us and took us down a flight of stairs and into the communal showers, where we were stripped and scrubbed. She rubbed awful-smelling stuff on our heads — to kill lice, she said. I did not have lice!

Then we were given clothes to put on, along with an apron. We were given a number that was written on all our clothing. When they lined us up, I noticed now that there were four other girls in front of us who must've arrived by another way. Then we went across to a small building, where a man was standing with scissors in his hand. Again we lined up and he cut our hair, the same as the rest of the girls that I had seen — straight across below the ears, and bangs. Then we went back inside and through a long hallway and up a flight of stairs.

We entered the girls' dorm. It was empty. There were three rows of beds. Light green curved metal head frames with three metal bars in between, and the same-coloured curved foot frames. There were metal night tables between the beds, of the same colour. The floor had smeared green tiles going one way, and the next row another way.

Like a checkerboard.

I was directed to the first row and to a bed that was the third from the end. There was a pile of stuff on the bed and there were lockers right across from the beds and that one was to be mine. I put the things that were on the bed into the locker. All the clothes had the number 75 written in black marker at the back of the neck, or on the tags at the back of the skirts. I was now #75. I wondered how many other girls had worn the #75 clothes.

As I closed the locker door, I turned and saw a girl in the tall mirror at the end of the room. She moved when I did and that was when I felt a shock go through me. That was me! I had never seen myself look like that before, and I began to shake and panic until I saw my eyes. There were my mother's eyes looking back at me. I was still me. They could do anything they wanted to me, but I would still be me!

All my own things are gone. Now I have to wear strange clothes and aprons with the number 75 on them. I am now just a number.

The Supervisor came in and directed us to follow her. We went down the stairs and stopped at a door and she led us in a prayer that we had to repeat after her. I never heard that prayer before. Then we entered the dining room, where all the girls were already eating. We were directed to empty chairs, and plates of food were put before us. I was very hungry. I just put my head down and began to eat. I can't even remember what we had for supper. The other new girl and I had to eat fast because the others couldn't leave until we were done. Then we had to say a thank-you prayer all together before we could leave the dining room. I didn't know this prayer either, so I had to just repeat what they were saying. The only prayers I ever heard were from the Bible when Grandma took me to the church sometimes at Flint Lake when the minister was there, which wasn't very often.

I have never watched television before. There was a cowboy show on in the evening. Then we were given some peanut-butter sandwiches and a glass of milk. Our Supervisor's name is Miss Tanner. She's an Anishinabe woman from down south somewhere. She is very cold though. She does not smile at all. She reminded me of a moving block of wood. She always seems to be looking around. I wonder what she's looking for.

Before the lights went off, we had to kneel

before our beds and say another prayer all together for bedtime. Again, we just have to say the same thing at the same time.

Saturday, September 10

After the wake-up bell rang, we all had to kneel by our beds for the morning prayer, and then we quickly had to make our beds before going into the washroom to wash and comb our hair and brush our teeth.

Miss Tanner showed me how to make my bed this morning. Tuck in the bottom sheet at the bottom and the top; lift the corners and tuck in and then tuck in the middle. She ripped off my first try and then I got it right the second time. It's like making a letter envelope.

The top is much the same. It has just a top sheet and a bed cover with the top folded over the pillow. We have to make our beds like that every morning so that all our beds look the same.

The bathroom sink is a thick round green stone circle thing. You step on the bottom metal circle ring and water sprays from the top mushroom-like thing. We each have a toothbrush and there's a container with minty powder in it that you stick your toothbrush into and it becomes toothpaste.

There are four toilet stalls by the wall. The doors and sides are about a foot from the floor so you can see the girls' feet when they go in. You can also look over the top if you stand on the toilet seat. I saw one of the girls do that. She must've been looking for someone.

I have an apron that I really like. I've never had one before. It has a white background with tiny yellow flowers and it has a gold-coloured trim around the collar and pockets, with ruffles around the sleeve straps and around the bottom. It's real pretty.

We have to wear white blouses and skirts and thick beige stockings.

Sunday, September 11

I forgot to mention that the boys all come into the dining room from another door and they all sit on one side of the room and we are not allowed to talk to them.

It's just now occurred to me how much trouble I'll be in if someone finds this diary. If someone sees me, they will certainly take it away from me. I have to be very careful. I'm thinking that it would be something I could read to Grandma when I get home to let her know what this place is like. Reading to her would be better than just giving it to her to read. I feel like we are kind of on this adventure together. I don't think I'd want my mother to see what I am writing, though, just in case my half-brother and half-sister end up in a place like this too. It would also remind her of the years that she spent in another Residential School when she was growing up. I'm thinking too much, I think.

I'm learning very quickly just to follow what the other girls are doing. If someone's not quite moving in the same direction at the same time, everyone stops and they glare at her. That was what they did to the other new girl beside me. So far, I've managed to keep up with what was happening. It reminds me of soldiers that I once saw in a book — all looking the same and all doing the same things at the same time. Even our dorm looks like an army's barracks. Before the lights go off, we have to say the night prayer all together for bedtime again. The prayer before meals is different from the after-meals prayer, and the bedtime prayer is also different, but we say them over and over again every day. I kept getting them mixed up yesterday.

This morning we had to pin little round lacy

things to the tops of our heads and then walk in a single file through a bush path. We walked through the bush slowly and it was so nice. Suddenly, one of the older girls tugged at my sweater. She had two new girls with her. She gestured for me to follow them. We ducked behind some bushes and she led us to a place where there were boulders jutting up from the ground. She said that we were not to forget this place because each new girl is told of this place. There are Residential School children buried there, she said. Then she told us it was now our duty to tell new girls of this place. I didn't see anything anywhere. Then, she turned and ran to catch up with the other girls. We looked at each other and we ran to catch up too.

The branches were still hanging on to a wide variety of leaves in bright colours of orange and yellow. It reminded me of home and I wished I could stay in the bush for a while, but I just took deep breaths and walked one foot in front of the other. It didn't smell the same though. There were many different trees and bushes that I didn't recognize.

We finally came to a clearing and there was a small Church. We went in line and sat in the rows at the back of the Church. We had to get up and sit down several times. It looked funny with all those people bobbing up and down together. I put my head down quick when I realized that I was smiling. I can't even remember what the white-gowned man with the ribbon stripe over his chest up front was saying. I was busy watching the white people, who largely ignored us, and I was admiring the different colours of glass on the pictures in the windows.

That was a boring long time in there. I kept thinking about the burial spot the girl showed us. I didn't see anything at all. Most graves I have seen had a mound or a cross or something. Maybe she was just pulling a joke on us.

This Church is very fancy. Not like the one at Flint Lake. I remember that I went in once when the bell rang as I was walking by on the way home to Grandma's, and it had a picture of Jesus beside the door and there were benches on each side of the aisle, and at the front was a table with a fancy cover that reached the floor and it had a cross on it. There was a little bench on the side, where the Minister knelt. I don't remember much about what the Minister said. He couldn't sing, either, and the women sang from the Cree hymn books they were using, since there were no Anishinabe books. That was funny. Mom and my stepfather, Izzy (I like that a lot better than his real name, Ezekiel) never went to the church on the Reserve. I never thought to ask why.

We each have jobs to do. I had to use the wax-buffing machine. It's a heavy green metal thing with a wide spinning brush at the end. It polishes the wax on the floor. I was told to plug it in, turn the switch up and go over the whole floor with it. Huh! It nearly knocked me off my feet when I first turned it on. It would have spun me around with it if I hadn't had the sense to keep my feet planted on the floor! Some of the girls were laughing at me struggling with the thing! I had to waltz around with it a couple of times before I figured out how to counter the right-hand pull of the spinning brush.

We watched *Walt Disney* after supper. Then *Bonanza* came on, with Little Joe in it. All the girls say that he's cute! *The Ed Sullivan Show* came on after that. I never saw any of those shows before. There was a television on the counter in a restaurant that I remember seeing on one of the trips into town with Mother. We'd get on the airplane and land in a small town to pick up some supplies or for one of us to see a doctor.

Tonight we had butter-and-jam sandwiches with our milk and then had to say the nighttime prayer before the lights went out.

Monday, September 12

Today was the first day of school. I didn't know where the school was, so I followed three girls, but then they turned into the park that is along the route. They began running, so I ran to catch up. They stopped at the foot of a huge tree and they asked me to come into its hollowed-out base with them. I was scared, but I joined them. I knew we were supposed to be at school, but how was I supposed to get there? I was very scared about going to a white city school for the first time in my life!

We sat there for a long time and they kept glancing around the tree. They said the caretaker would chase us out of the park if he saw us. We wriggled around to fit in that big gaping hole and we sat there huddled and they whispered once in a while. It was very damp and a cold mist was still on the ground. I was getting very cold. Then I think I must have dozed off, because one girl poked me and they were glancing up the street, saying that the kids were coming back. I was wearing a blue sweater, but it was still cold outside and I was shivering.

We knew it must be lunchtime when we saw the others coming back down the street, and we sort of walked along on the other side of the street and joined the last straggling kids back to the Residential School. We then lined up with the others at the dining-room door. When we were all there, Miss Tanner kept order and we all said the grace and then we were allowed to take our seats at the tables and silently ate our meal. After the meal, we had to say the thank-you prayer. There's no talking allowed at mealtimes, and we have to eat everything on the plate. I really don't care what I eat. I just eat what's put in front of me.

After lunch, our names were called through the intercom to come to the office. That is, me and the other three girls. We were asked to wait outside the office and we were called in one by one. When it was my turn, the Principal glared at me and gave me a big loud lecture about playing hooky. I didn't even know what "hooky" meant! Then, he asked if I knew where the school was. I shook my head. Then he said that I must go to school every day and I was never to spend the day in the park again!

I hate this place!

Tuesday, September 13

I just remembered Tall Mike. He had told me that he failed on purpose because his dad needs him at home. So, he'll have to keep failing Grade 5 so that he can stay home until he's old enough to leave school. I wonder how old he'd have to be? I think I should have done that too. Then I could have stayed with Grandma forever.

The city school that we go to is called King George and I was kind of scared. I've never been in a school with white kids before. They were all right though. They just stared at me at first, and the teachers were very nice. I am the only Anishinabe girl out of about 25 students in my first morning class. I saw some girls from the Residential School in some of the classes, but they don't talk to anyone, not even me.

It's almost time for supper. I wonder what we'll have this evening. Yesterday it was chili with mashed potatoes and carrots. I think I'll write down what we eat so that I'll know what it's called when I tell Grandma about the different food we eat.

Wednesday, September 14

We move to different classes for different subjects at school. It's not so boring because you don't sit in one spot all day long. I just stand by the door at recess. The white girls stand together talking, and the boys spend the time wrestling and punching each other, or chasing each other around the yard. No one talks to me and no one bothers me. I don't mind. I don't feel like talking to anyone, and I'm just feeling very lonely and wish I was home with Grandma! I wonder how Mother felt, to be able to go to school in the Residential School where she lived and not have to go to a town school with white kids.

I decided to go to the park after supper and a girl came running after me from the Residential School. She must have just arrived. She had bright red fingernails. She flashed a smile and started talking. She kept talking the whole time it took to get to the candy shop at the park, and she talked all the way back too. She talked about *everything*, and finally, just before we went back inside the Residential School, she made me promise that I would meet her in Paris on her honeymoon. I wasn't quite sure where Paris was!

Thursday, September 15

After class, I was walking down the hallway at school on my way out and I met the English teacher. He asked me what it looks like where I come from. I didn't know if I should tell him about the Reserve or Flint Lake. I thought I'd tell him about Flint Lake and Grandma. It was a lot easier telling him about the railroad and trains, the store and the school. He was surprised when I told him that there were no roads and no cars. He asked if I liked coming to a city like this. I shook my head and told him I'd rather be at home. He laughed. Maybe he thought I was joking.

Friday, September 16

We were given ski jackets this morning. They were all hanging on a rack by the side entrance that we use. It is just outside the dining-room door. Someone said that it was once a playroom, but it's quite empty now except for the coat rack and the boot trays that line the wall beside the door. The one that fit me is light green and Miss Tanner put #75 on the back collar with a marker. The winter boots that fit me looked like old-white-lady boots with the lace-up fronts. I didn't care as long as my feet were warm. It was all second-hand clothing anyway. I noticed the girl — Paris, as I call her in my head. Her red nail polish was gone and she had a sad look. She smiled at a few girls but didn't say very much to anyone.

I wrote a letter to Grandma. I don't know if they will mail it. We have to hand in our letters at the office and they read them before they send them, if they send them. When there's a letter for us, it's opened and read, and if it is okay, they give it to us. We are not allowed to say anything about the Residential School when we write home.

Anyway, there wasn't much I had to say.

In case they don't mail my letter, I'll write it here too, so Grandma can see it when I get home.

September 16, 1966
Insy Pimash
Flint Lake, Ontario
Hello, Grandma.

I know you are probably setting your fishnet for trout. I wish I could be there with you. We got four of the trout that time in the pouring rain when we checked the fishnet. Remember that your kerchief was so soaked you decided to wring it out and wipe your face with it? That was funny. We made a lot of use of your old canoe last fall. I hope Mother and Izzy figure out how to get you a new one next summer. I remember you saying that your old canoe is so full of patches that it's only the patches that are holding it together. I hope someone is helping you put in a store of wood enough for the winter.

I am fine and everything is okay. I do very much miss you. I miss your morning list of things to do while you put the wood in the stove. There was always the things that had to be done before the sun set. I have not heard from Mother yet. I hope she will write soon. Write back to me real soon too. I love you very much.

Love,
Violet (Pynut)

Saturday, September 17

Miss Lewis is our Supervisor on the weekends when Miss Tanner takes a break. I like her. She is a lot more friendly than the other one. She has brown hair and blue eyes and is very short. She's the same height as me! I really like her.

Some of the girls wash dishes after meals. The older ones are in the laundry room, ironing all our stuff. There are some that are in charge of mending our clothes. So far, I have been just sweeping the dining-room floor and buffing the dorm floor. I haven't actually shampooed or polished the floor yet. The older girls do that. I saw Paris and asked her if she would like to go to the park afterward, but she just shook her head.

There was a bit of a blowout with the boys that we heard about. Apparently, one of the boys swiped one of the pies that the cook had cooling on the windowsills outside the kitchen. All the girls were laughing about that. We don't know if they figured out which one did it. One of the girls said that if the boys refuse to tell, they all get punished.

Oh, when I was going over the floor with the wax-buffing machine this morning, I noticed a cigarette lying on the floor against the night table between two beds. I didn't know which girl it belonged to, but I quickly picked it up and shoved it under the corner of the sheet on the bed to the right and continued with the machine. I don't know if anyone saw me. There were two girls at the other end, dusting around the windows. There were also girls coming and going in the washroom, cleaning the place.

At bedtime, I glanced over to the two beds just in time to see the girl on the right pull up the sheet, and the cigarette flew out, landed on the floor and rolled toward the Supervisor's feet! Everyone stopped dead. Some craned their necks to see what had happened, and soon every eye was on that cigarette. Miss Lewis stood there for a while before she pointed at it and asked whose cigarette that was. The two girls looked at each other and both said, "not mine." Miss Lewis picked it up and put it in her pocket and everyone continued what they were doing.

Sunday, September 18

Just before the breakfast bell rang, the two girls were called to the office. I don't know what happened to them, but I didn't see them at breakfast. I don't feel bad about putting the cigarette inside the girl's sheet because it must have belonged to one of them. I was just trying to keep the girl from getting into trouble. If Miss Lewis hadn't been standing there at the time, it would have been all right.

We actually did get a slice of apple pie after supper, but we were wondering if the boys got any. I couldn't see if they did. The plates were cleared away so fast, we didn't get a chance to whisper to any of the boys who were clearing their dishes, before they were ushered out. I recognized the boys' Supervisor as the one who picked us up from the train station the day we arrived. I hadn't noticed him before. He has a loud, booming voice, so I have certainly heard him many times.

We didn't have to pin the lacy things to the tops of our heads this morning. We just marched in line to the Chapel at the end of the field in front of the Residential School. We had to listen to the Principal talk about one thing or another. Sing songs, stand up and sit down, and then march our way back to the Residential School and wait for the lunch bell.

I really have to get my homework done this afternoon though. It has to do with a moose, for the Science class. I don't know much about moose. Izzy killed moose, but he was always hunting with the other guys on the Reserve and brought back the meat. Grandma never hunted moose, but some of the men at Flint Lake would give her a piece of meat whenever they killed one. There are no books here, so I had to bring back some books from the King George School library that teach things about moose.

Monday, September 19

I got a letter from Mother. And, it had a five-dollar bill inside! I am going to save it and only buy some candy or a chocolate on Saturdays.

I don't know if we get to keep our letters. Maybe they take them away after, so I am going to write down what the letter says so that I can read it over again.

September 10th
Hello daughter,

I have managed to get a job as the Secretary at the Band Office! Thank goodness for the course I took over the summer! Now we have a bit more money coming in for the house. Your brother and sister are doing fine. They like their new teacher at school. The Band also got funding for a construction project that your father is signed up to work at. There is also a new Chief now and your father also campaigned to be one of the Councillors and he actually won one of the seats! So, things are looking up. He is now one of the Councillors! Please write as soon as you can and let me know you are all right. I do worry about you and hope you are all right. I write and call your

grandma whenever I can, so you will know that
we know that you are okay.

Your mother,
Emily

Tuesday, September 20

My two friends — Laura and Susan — and I went to the park on the way home from school. Laura has a little brother in the Residential School too. We see him sometimes on the way to school. He just waves at her. He runs off with the other boys every time she tries to talk to him. She says that the boys tease him if he's caught talking to his sister.

There's a guy at the park who has a little shed thing and he stands behind the counter and sells newspapers and candy. I had the five-dollar bill in my pocket and I bought a sponge toffee bar. Oh, it was good. I had to share it with my friends though. That was okay.

Susan told me to ignore the white girls at school who won't talk to me. I didn't even realize that they were deliberately ignoring me! I thought they were just being nice by not bothering me. I am dumb for sure, maybe. I'm just getting used to being in classrooms with white students. I never used to think about myself being Anishinabe, but now I'm always remembering who I am when they look at me like I'm not supposed to be there.

I feel like I am invading their space.

Wednesday, September 21

The Monkees were on the television this evening. Davy's cute! I secretly think the show is kind of silly, but the other girls really like watching it. We got peanut-butter sandwiches with apple juice tonight. That was nice. I heard some girls saying that there's nothing else for comfort here but food. Some of the older girls were saying that they get fat in the winter when they are here, but lose all that weight when they go home for the summer because there is always more work, and there's not always food to eat back home. That's one thing that I had never thought about. I was never hungry with Mother on the Reserve, or with Grandma. Though Mother sometimes talked about being hungry, or about the bad food, when *she* was at Residential School.

I didn't know that I was a very lucky girl. There's one thing I notice too. There's always the smell of food cooking in here, and I do eat whatever is put in front of me because I know I'd get into trouble if I didn't eat it. But then I haven't tasted anything I didn't like here yet.

Thursday, September 22

I wrote to Mother this afternoon and gave the letter to Miss Tanner. I hope they send it to her.

If not, I can read this copy to her when I see her.

September 22, 1966
Dear Mother,

I'm doing fine and I like watching television. I had no idea there were so many things to watch on the television. I'm watching The Monkees, and Bonanza with Little Joe in it. The girls think he is cute! Then there is Walt Disney, which is a movie about stories of dogs, or children, or other animal stories. Then there is an Ed Sullivan Show where he brings people onto the stage. Sometimes there are people with tricks, animals that can do tricks, or people telling jokes, or most times, some famous bands and singers.

The food is good. I didn't know there were so many kinds of food and I found a sponge toffee that I never tasted before and it's really good.

Thank you for the money and I will make it last as long as I can. Give my love to my brother and sister. Say hello to Izzy for me. I hope I will see you all at Christmas. It is only September and all the girls are already talking about going home for Christmas.

I wrote a letter to Grandma and I hope I hear from her soon.

Your daughter,
Violet

Saturday, September 24

I went for a walk after lunch to see the neighbourhood. I don't know where the rest of the girls went, because I had a bath first. I went in the other direction this time and started looking around so that I didn't get lost. I noticed a large red STOP sign at the end of the street. Well, I thought I couldn't miss that. So I went down the street and walked up another street. There was a grocery store down another street. I could see the sign, so I went to check it out. It was a small grocery store at the corner and it sold all kinds of things. I bought another chocolate bar that I'd never seen before. It was coconut and covered with chocolate. It was too sweet. Didn't like it much. I went back the way I came and was happy to see the STOP sign, but when I got there, it didn't look anything like the street that had the STOP sign on it.

I turned around and went in another direction, and soon I spotted another STOP sign. I was so happy that I ran toward it, but when I got there, I had never seen *this* street before either! I had no idea there were so many STOP signs!!! I didn't know what to do and I was getting scared, so I figured if the sun is to the west, then I should walk with it to my right. I came to a busy street and I saw a bus go by before I came to the corner and then I recognized the park across the street. I was so thirsty by that time, I ran all the way back to Residential School and I got in just in time because the girls were lining up for supper already!

Sunday, September 25

We didn't have to go to the Church through the bush today either — the one with the white people there, and the Minister. We just went to the Chapel at the far end of the school grounds. The Principal talked for a bit and we sang some songs. Then we came back and then it was lunchtime. Boring morning! I have to do my homework this afternoon. Yuck! I hate it! I hate it! I hate it!

I want to go home so badly! I still have not heard from Grandma.

Emma came to see me this afternoon. I had to meet her outside though. She didn't want to come in. My friend Susan came and got me. They were all playing outside when Emma arrived. I ran downstairs, grabbed my jacket and there she was leaning against the building. We walked to the park. She says that she likes the house where she's staying along with two other girls. She likes the high school she's going to. She was asking me about how I like this place, but I didn't want to talk about the Residential School. After walking around a bit, she left to catch the bus and I ran back. Just in time too! I didn't know what time it was and I just barely got my jacket and boots off when the supper bell rang and all the girls trooped down the stairs and we all lined up. If you miss the lineup, you miss the meal.

Monday, September 26

I really liked the movie on *Walt Disney* last night. It was about a dog and he was really smart. I didn't know what to write today. That movie gave me an idea and so I decided to write a story about Blackie, my friend from Flint Lake.

Title: *BLACKIE OF FLINT LAKE* by Violet Pesheens

Blackie lives in a place called Flint Lake.

He's a big, bushy, black dog and he always barks at people when they walk by.

One day, the new girl walked by on her way to school. He used to see her with the old woman at the end of the path, but now she always walks by alone.

One day, he decided to bark at her to see what she would do. But she didn't do anything and just ignored him. So he decided to bark louder and follow her, barking all the while.

Still she did not pay any attention to him. That made him mad so he barked some more and then she laughed at him. That made him angrier so he barked longer and more loudly. Still she went on walking.

I don't think this is going to work. It is boring. Maybe I can add another dog.

One day, there was a new dog. It was a big, beige, male dog who always sat on the hill and watched the girl walk by.

Oh, the supper bell just rang. The girls are dropping what they are doing.

Time to line up.

Tuesday, September 27

I wrote to Grandma again and gave her the address to this place again. I hope they mail it. I'll copy it out here too, so that I can read it to Grandma when I get home.

Sept. 27, Tuesday
Insy Pimash
Flint Lake, Ontario
Dear Grandma,

I'm doing well. I just wanted to make sure that you know the address to this place. I copied the address from Mother's letter to me that was dated September 10th.

I'm learning new things at school. I didn't know anything about Geography. I wonder why the teacher at Flint Lake didn't tell us about that. I can do Math and English really well, so there's no problem there. There's also History that I find really interesting.

We have different teachers for the different subjects. They're all very nice. The other students don't bother me and they sure dress differently from us. The white girls have bright red painted toenails and some are still wearing sandals. They have fancy skirts and dresses.

Their hair is always curled or in little bobs that look like caps on their heads. The boys still dress the same as all boys do.

Emma came to visit me on Sunday. She likes where she's living. She lives with a family of four. The mother, father, a boy and a girl about her own age. They all go to the same high school. There are two other Anishinabe girls living there too.

I noticed that there are strange squirrels here. They are black and very big with big bushy tails! There are strange birds too. I don't know what they are called. I have to look for pictures of them at the King George School library. That's the city school we go to. There's a calendar at the school that has all the holidays written on it. I never knew there were so many special days for stuff.

Please write to me when you have time. I love you and miss you very much.

Yours,
Violet (Pynut)

I had a cry by the window. I wonder why Grandma hasn't written to me yet? I was looking out the window, watching the snow come down, and another girl came to stand beside me, and then she began to cry too when she saw me crying. Soon, there were four of us crying, when Miss Tanner saw us. She ordered us away from the window. She was very angry! Nasty crow! I don't know why she works here if she's not happy. I have yet to see her smile.

Wednesday, September 28

It was really cold going to school this morning. Freezing rain and very windy. We had snow a couple of times, but it didn't stay on the ground.

I always feel this hopeless pain or longing in my chest — to go home — and I feel hopeless that I can't and there's nothing I can do about it.

I just finished a pencil drawing of Grandma's cabin. I even put in her washtub that's always hanging on the side of the cabin outside, her sawhorse and a pile of wood.

Thursday, September 29

I'm sitting under the window. I can smell something delicious cooking from the kitchen downstairs. I might get tired of the breakfast food. It's either salty porridge or cream of wheat with one piece of toast. But, I'm not complaining. At least I'm not hungry.

I don't know where the girls are. I seem to be up here by myself. The younger girls are probably still running around outside. The older girls hang out in the bushes at the back of the building. I could see some boys out there too, when I looked out the back fire-escape window when I came in from school.

I got a string about 2 feet long from the Science room at King George yesterday. We were standing around by the windows, waiting for the supper bell to ring, when I remembered it. I tied the ends together and I began playing the string games that everybody knows back home. I saw a girl nearby and I stuck out the criss-crossed string to her, and without a word, she immediately turned it into another figure. Then another girl joined us and she turned it into another figure and then a Cree girl joined us and she knew the game too!

We were not speaking, but just smiling at each other, when one of the older girls walked by and she just reached out and grabbed the string and, glancing around, hissed, "Are you girls *stupid*?" stuck it into her apron pocket and ran down the stairs. I asked one of the girls, "What's wrong?" She sighed and said, "We were playing our game — like our language, not allowed. I forgot too."

I don't understand. It was just a *game*. I *hate* this place!!

It snowed a bit. Seeing that made me very homesick. I remember the fun Grandma and I used to have hauling wood in the snow. I wish I was home with Grandma. I just want to go home!!!

Friday, September 30

We were really cold on the way to school. Freezing rain and strong winds!

We have to wear skirts. I wish they'd let us wear pants when it's cold like this!

We were all in bed in the dark last night after the Supervisor shut off the lights.

There's a girl two beds down from me. She was trying not to forget the Lord's Prayer in Anishinabe and she said "shigag shigag" for "forever and ever." That means "skunk skunk" in our language. The words for "forever and ever" should be "kagiga kagiga." That was really funny! Although she was the only one speaking out loud, we were actually following along with her. That's why we burst out loud laughing into our pillows when she said "skunk skunk."

It was a good thing that the Supervisor did not hear us. I wonder how the girl would have explained that one. I know the Lord's Prayer in our language because Grandma taught me. Her mother taught it to her. My mother doesn't know it though.

Saturday, October 1

We have different jobs to do now. The duty roster is taped beside the door. I am on dorm- and stairway-sweeping duty. I use a wide push broom for the dorm and a small broom and dust- pan for the stairway. One girl tried to step on my hand when she came running down the stairs, but I was too quick.

We had meatloaf, gravy, mashed potatoes and carrots for supper. Yum!

I ask what the meal is called if I really like it. They don't give us seconds, which is a good thing. Otherwise I would be a very fat girl by the time I leave!

That's funny because I never used to care what I ate as long as my tummy had some food in it. Grandma cooks better than Mother, I know that.

I remember my stepfather, Izzy, saying that all Mother could do was boil or fry food when they first got married. I don't know that her cooking has improved! But whatever she makes, there's always a lot of it.

I just realized that maybe I have been too hard on Izzy. Just because my mother married him doesn't mean she pushed me aside. Izzy works hard and he's a very gentle man. He never raises his voice to us and he's always very cheerful.

Yeah, I think it was me that made the home at the Reserve not always happy. I just never fit in because Mother and I have always lived with Grandma at Flint Lake until she met and married Izzy.

I'm getting tired. I'm going to go to bed now. I didn't like the movie on television tonight so I decided to write this instead.

Sunday, October 2

We got a boiled egg each this morning with toast. That was nice.

My Blackie story is coming along fine. I added in that part about when Blackie saved me from the big trapper's dog that broke his chain and attacked me on my way home from the store.

Blackie charged up and got him off me, but poor Blackie got the bad end of that fight before his owner came to the rescue. I changed it a bit from what actually happened and it made a little better story, I think.

I have the story in the same kind of paper as my diary — school writing paper cut in four. I tie the pages together with thread. I went into the sewing room one day when the girls were in there mending clothes. One of the older Anishinabe girls took my papers and ran them through on the sewing machine! Now I just fold the paper in half, she sews the middle, and there, I have a little notebook!

Monday, October 3

When we got back after school, a screaming fight broke out in the washroom. Two girls were screaming at each other in Anishinabe and everyone cleared out quickly.

I could understand them but I couldn't make any sense of what they were yelling about, when suddenly Miss Tanner rushed into the washroom and ushered them out and down the stairs to the office.

I asked the girl beside me what they were going

to do to them. She just looked at me and said "strap." I hear it's a yardstick that the Principal uses to punish people who do something wrong — we are strictly not allowed to use our own language in this place. English only.

Which reminds me, I thought I was pretty good with my English, and writing in particular. But I'm discovering that I'm not as good as I thought I was. My English papers keep coming back from the teacher with great red marks and Xs. I can't figure out what is wrong with my writing most of the time. I don't know what I'm doing wrong.

Tuesday, October 4

There was a beige dog running flat out around the park when we were coming home from school. It kept running back and forth, and several times it ran toward us and then it would run back to the park again. I think it was really panicked and lost. Poor dog. I just started crying. It reminded me of Jennie's first dog, Chuck. It was really sad when he got hit by a train and died.

An Indian Affairs doctor came to the school to check us over. We had to go in one by one and come out through another door. I was walking behind some older girls and I overheard one girl saying that the doctor had touched her in places that she didn't think had anything to do with a medical checkup. But they shut up when they noticed me behind them. I don't know what that was about.

It's getting really cold walking to and from school with our skirts on. I don't know why they will not let us wear pants!

Wednesday, October 5

I really liked lunch today. The cook made toast with melted cheese on top with a slice of bacon on the top of that and some soup. That was yummy!!!

It was my turn to sweep the dining-room floor. There were two of us, so we were done pretty fast and we ran almost all the way back to school. I could have run all the way, but she got tuckered out just past the park.

It was cold today with our dresses on. We are not allowed to wear slacks. I think I have repeated that several times already! I think I wrote that down yesterday too!

We take turns using the showers, but there are bathtubs in the basement too. I decided to take a bath after supper. There was no one around. I took my time floating around in the nice warm water, since there was no one waiting for me. It made me think of Grandma. She used to heat up the water and pour it into the washtub and it was just big enough for me to squat down into it, and she'd wash my hair and back with the wood stove popping away in the corner. I really miss Grandma.

Thursday, October 6

The two girls I usually walk home with after school were already by the main street when I came out. I was walking along, thinking about a project I had to do, when a car pulled up beside me. The man rolled down the window and told me to get in and he would take me for a ride. He was a balding, fat white man and I had never seen him before. I began to run, but he kept pace with me. The two girls up ahead had stopped to talk about something and I finally caught up with them and the car turned a corner.

I told the girls what the man said. One girl continued walking but the older girl asked me if I got the number of the car. I looked at her, puzzled, and asked, "What number?" She sighed and said, "The number of the car. Each car has a different number and the number is on the front and back. What colour was it?" I said, "Light blue?" Then she shook her head at me. "If that ever happens again, take down the number and the colour of the car and get a good look at the driver and write it down." I asked why? She took one long look at me and said, "So the police have something to go on if something happens to you!" I blinked. "What do you mean 'If something happens to me'?" Then she just leaned over and told me, "You are *stupid*!" and ran off to catch up with her friend.

I am sitting under the window now and I still do not understand one bit of that talk.

Right after that, though, I saw a car coming and looked for numbers and I saw some on the white square below the car. When the car went by, sure enough, there was another white square on the back with the same number! Then I saw light flashing on the right side and then the car turned right. Another car went by and it had different numbers on the square. It had a light flashing on the left and the car turned left! I hadn't noticed the cars at all the whole time I have been here.

After supper, when I was sweeping the dining-room floor, I asked one of the older girls about the man in the car, and she told me that sometimes bad men throw girls in the car and drive them somewhere far, and hurt them really bad or kill them. That's why I should always look around me and try not to walk alone.

I had no idea danger came from people in cars. I knew that a car will kill you if it hits you, but I did not know a driver was dangerous too!

Friday, October 7

I really enjoyed supper this evening. Yum, yum! Spaghetti and meatballs.

There are two Cree girls who always wait at the corner of the school at the end of the day, and they follow behind me, chanting and chanting in Cree. I don't know what they are saying because I can't understand them. Then this afternoon, they were on the street sidewalk, holding hands and blocking my way. I thought to turn around and go the other way around the block, but I'm getting really angry at them. So instead I started running right toward them as fast as I could and I crashed right against their hands flat out. I heard them smack against each other. I glanced back and one girl was leaning over with her hand over her face, blood dripping between her fingers, and I kept running. I ran all the way back. I'm sitting in the corner by the window now, pretending to be doing my homework. They are not in the dorm right now. I hate this place!

I get very angry sometimes and I don't know why. It's like a burning pain across my chest. I never used to get angry. I remember only once two winters ago when my brother Lyndon got into my box where I keep a set of embroidered hankies that Grandma gave me, and he had blown his nose on all of them. I don't remember getting angry since. Now I'm angry all the time.

Saturday, October 8

It was my turn to sweep the dining-room floor after lunch. The other girl was a big Cree girl who seems not to like me, for some reason. I don't even know her, but she tried to trip me with her broom. I noticed a group of Cree girls that are very mean and they pick on new girls like me, but there are three older Anishinabe girls who are always nearby when they show up. So I haven't been beaten up yet. I *have* seen some of the new girls with bleeding lips or scratches on their faces. I just try to stay out of everyone's way and try to be nice to everyone. I smiled at a girl across the table from me at lunch and she just stuck her tongue out at me. Oh well.

I just finished adding Grandma coming around the corner of her cabin on my sketch. She is carrying a paper box from the store.

Sunday, October 9

I'm sitting under the front window where I usually sit. I'm just waiting for the lunch bell to ring. Service was at the Chapel this morning and it was boring again today. I like the colourful windows though. I just have to get up when everyone gets up and then sit down when everyone else does. Then we march back to the Residential School. It is a big brown brick building. I think I forgot to mention that at the beginning. It's a large brick building with a row of windows on each floor. It is three stories high with an attic on top and—

Oh, that was close! I looked up to see Miss Lewis come in and I just had time to switch my diary to my Blackie story I had beneath it. She came to see what I was writing, so I read her some parts. She thought it was really funny when I read her the part about Blackie running into a frozen block of wood buried under the newly fallen snow.

I am sitting facing the door, so I just have to remember to look up once in a while.

Emma never showed up again. She must be busy.

Monday, October 10

It is Thanksgiving Day today.

I'm not really sure what that means. Maybe it is just a day to be thankful for everything. Then I think they should just call it Thankful Day.

I never knew so many holidays existed. We had a special supper of turkey slices, mashed potatoes, gravy and stuffing. We even had a small piece of pumpkin pie each.

Back home, nobody pays attention to the holidays marked on the calendar.

Oh, I forgot. Last week, the teacher asked me a question about something on the board and I just shook my head. After school, he told me to stay at my desk and asked why I didn't answer the question, because he knew that I knew the answer. So I told him I didn't know which question he was talking about. He went to the board and wrote something and came back to me and asked me what it said. I told him I didn't know, because I couldn't see what he wrote from where I was sitting. He just shook his head.

Tuesday, October 11

An older Anishinabe girl and I were sent to a dentist's office in town this afternoon, but I didn't know where we were supposed to go. The girl stopped at the door of a large building, but then she decided to go to the Kresge's store instead. I told the Supervisor when we got back, so that I didn't get into trouble. So Miss Lewis is going to take me next week instead. I have a back tooth that needs a filling. Back home, the dentist who came to the school just pulled out our teeth. This will be my first filling.

When we got back to the Residential School, Miss Tanner handed me a letter. It was from Grandma!

This is what Grandma said.

October 4, 1966
Hello, Pynut,

I got your letter and I really do miss you too. Jennie ended up going home to her hometown, her dog Lucy with her. She is staying with her mother's sister to go to the school they have there. I don't know her address, but if you would like, I will ask her mother for it.

There is nothing going on here, as you will remember, nothing ever does. Blackie sits by his doorstep and I do believe he is really sad that you are not around anymore. He always looks disappointed when I come around the corner all by myself. There is a new teacher at the school this year. She is a rather big blond woman with her hair always pinned in a big bun at the back of her head. Several children are coming home with bruises from her hitting them with whatever she can get her hands on. I am glad you are no longer there.

Please keep writing whenever you can and I will answer whenever I can get to the store. Sometimes the snow is so deep, I have to wait until someone makes a track to the store. The young man down the way, Rob, says he will make a path to the railway tracks for me with

*his snowshoes. You remember the couple with
the new baby? That will make it easier for me.
At least the trains clear the snow on the tracks.*

*Take care of yourself and remember I love
you always with all my heart.*

Grandma

Grandma only mentions one letter. I have
written her *two* letters already. I wonder which
one she got?

Wednesday, October 12

A girl refused to eat her supper and she had to
sit there until she did. She was still sitting there
crying when we finished sweeping the floor.
The other girls said that it was beef goulash or
something. I just ate it. It tasted kind of like sour
cream, but I ate it. I haven't been punished yet for
not eating my food.

I'm answering Grandma's letter instead of
watching television this evening.

If Grandma is not getting all my letters, I must
be sure to copy everything into my diary.

Wednesday, October 12, 1966
Insy Pimash
Flint Lake, Ontario
Dear Grandma,

It was so good to hear from you. Yes, please ask for Jennie's address. I do miss her and Lucy too. I'm doing fine and things are all right, other than that I miss you and the cabin. I am learning some new stuff at school and I discovered that I really love watching television in the evenings. I have seen a television, of course, when I was at the hospital or at the Band Office on the Reserve, but I didn't know about all the evening shows they have here. There are shows for children and comedy for adults and then there are the cowboy shows and new music band shows. We also have a snack of sandwiches and milk while we watch the shows before bed. The meals are good too. That's all you smell when you come in the side door where we come and go, since it's just off the dining room and the kitchen just beyond that. It is a comforting smell and makes you very hungry.

There was a big storm last night. We could hear the wind howling around the windows *and see the snow hitting the windowpanes. I was thinking of you, and if you have storms like that I hope you are snug and warm inside your little cabin. I miss Blackie too. I started writing a story about Blackie. It is getting quite thick. I put him in all kinds of adventures and he rescues people and drags drowning kids to shore and then he gets into fights with other dogs. I am going to draw a picture of him on the cover when I am done.*

I wish I was there with you. It's two more months before I can see you again. I can't wait! We will go rabbit snaring and ice fishing with the little toboggan pulled behind us.

With all my love,
Violet (Pynut) Pesheens

Thursday, October 13

The big Cree girl was sweeping the dining-room floor after lunch, and when I went to get the broom from the closet, she came in and grabbed it from me. I need a broom to sweep the floor quick or I will be late for school. She wouldn't give it to me, so I just lunged and grabbed it from her. She held on, so I threw her to the floor and still she would not let go of the broom, so I pushed the handle against her throat and I put both my knees on both sides. I felt a hot, searing anger come over me. I never felt this kind of anger in my whole life before! I didn't know I was that strong either! I worked hard with Grandma cutting wood and hauling water, so I guess I have a lot of muscles.

Anyway, I watched her face turn red and she couldn't breathe, but I wouldn't let her go until I heard someone coming. I jumped up and grabbed the broom and went out and began sweeping the floor. I could hear the girl coughing and gasping. When I finished sweeping and put the broom back, she was gone.

After supper

I was expecting to be called to the office for some kind of punishment, ever since we came home from school, but nothing yet. I guess I'll just keep waiting. I wish they would just get it over with. I started shaking when I was thinking of what they would do to me. It's bedtime soon. Maybe the Cree girl didn't say anything.

Friday, October 14

I waited for my punishment for beating up the Cree girl before breakfast, but still nothing.

At lunch, I swept the floor and saw that girl sweeping up her half of the dining room without looking at me. I ran all the way back to King George School.

After supper, I went to the washroom and found blood on my panties. Grandma had told me that this would happen, but I didn't know what to do, so I went to Miss Tanner and she took me upstairs, where she gave me an elastic strap to put around my waist, and it had clips hanging down at the front and back. Then she gave me a package of pads with long tails at each end. I stood there holding one tail, trying to figure out how I was supposed to put the thing on. She sighed and told me that these pad ends are what slip through the clips hanging down from the waist strap. It really is a weird-looking thing. I was very dismayed that this would happen every month for one whole week!

Oh, I wish I was home with Grandma. I cried before I could come down the stairs. I want Mother and Grandma! I want to go home!

Saturday, October 15

The big Cree girl just ignores me now. The other two girls haven't bothered me again either.

Miss Lewis asked me to come with her after supper. We went down the hall and into an empty room with a bed in it, and she told me to lie down on the bed. She said she's studying to be a nurse and she has to learn how to change the sheets without moving me. We laughed a lot as she tried to follow instructions from a book. She had to do it four times before she got it right. Then one more time to make sure she could do it quick. That was fun!

While I was there, and since she was going to be a nurse, I mentioned about my cramps and wondered if I had to put up with the pain and the blood too every month! I told her it seemed like very unjust punishment to me. She laughed and gave me an Aspirin, saying that she could only give them to me one at a time and only when the cramps got real bad.

Sunday, October 16

Emma came this afternoon. She was very happy. We walked to the park again and we talked about home. She says that her brother

Mike wrote to tell her that her little sister got sick and had to go to the hospital, but that she is okay now. Otherwise, everyone is fine at home. Except an old man called Ol' Moses had an accident and died. I felt very bad about that. I remember on January 1st he showed up at Grandma's cabin for the "hugs and kisses" day, when people went around from cabin to cabin hugging and kissing each other. I remember Grandma and I went ice fishing right after he left, because we didn't want anyone else coming for hugs and kisses — Grandma knew I didn't like it.

Emma didn't know exactly what happened to him. Maybe Grandma will say something about him the next time she writes.

Monday, October 17

I was in the washroom, washing my face before supper, when I heard someone sobbing in one of the toilet cubicles. There are four toilets against one wall. There's a space below the door and I could see her feet. I asked her what was wrong. She didn't answer. So I went into the toilet beside her and I stepped up on the toilet seat and peered over the wall. She was sitting with her hands over her face. It was Sandra, one of the Cree girls. She had scratches on her face. I asked what happened to her. She looked up and then opened the door and came out. I helped her wash her face.

She looked like someone punched her in the face too. She finally told me that her friend Angie had a boyfriend back home, who is now at the Residential School too. Sandra saw him outside after school and they started talking. Angie came out of the school and saw them and Angie just attacked her. I think Sandra's going to have a black eye. I'm going to remember never to tangle with Angie.

Tuesday, October 18

I took a peek into the laundry room across from the dining room after supper today. The girls were there ironing the clothes. I don't know which ones do the laundry, but the ones who were ironing were the Cree girls who used to bother me. I smiled and they smiled back at me.

I just realized that I have not seen Sandra.

Wednesday, October 19

We had meatloaf, carrots and mashed potatoes for supper, and when we were back in the dorm, one of the older girls said that the

Supervisors, the Boss — that's what everyone calls the Principal — and the other people who ran the place eat different food than us. I wonder what they ate that was different. I really didn't mind the food we got. I really don't care. They can eat whatever they like I guess.

Thursday, October 20

Miss Lewis took me to the dentist this afternoon. We took the bus there and back.

She showed me the address of the dentist's office, and that got me thinking, so I asked her how a city address worked. I only need to put "General Delivery" and the town when I write a letter to Mother and Grandma. That's when she told me that all streets have different names and all the houses and buildings have numbers on them. So when we got to town, she showed me the street sign and then she made me find the building number. That was fun!

The dentist was nice and the filling wasn't too bad. My lip was frozen on one side all afternoon. But, I was all right by suppertime. Miss Lewis was really nice to be with.

Friday, October 21

Sandra, the Cree girl, was back at her place at the dining-room table this evening. She still has a black eye. I don't know where she was for the last couple of days. They don't let us talk about anything, and no one tells us anything, so we don't know anything about anything!

Saturday, October 22

I bought another sponge toffee from the man at the park this afternoon. This time I was by myself, so I got to eat it all by myself!

There was hardly anyone around at the park today. It was cold and windy. That candy man said something weird to me. He never says anything, but today he said if I came back at five o'clock, he would give me a free chocolate bar. I didn't like the way he was looking at me, from my feet to my head. I did not like that look. I don't think I will be going there again. I discovered a small corner store down the street before the Residential School. I can just run there on the way home. There was no one in the dorm when I got back.

I am going to write a letter to Jennie, I think. I will try to mail it whenever I find out where to send it. I'll read my letters from Grandma and Mother first. I'm feeling very homesick.

Later

I'm sitting under the front window right now. I went to reach for my letters from Mother and Grandma, but they weren't there! Someone has *taken* my letters! I had them on the top shelf of my locker, under some clothes. I've been crying since. Now, I won't even see their handwriting anymore. It's a good thing I copied the letters down here, but it's still not the same.

Sunday, October 23

We all trooped to the Chapel this morning. It was very foggy. The boys were running around in the field until the Supervisor bellowed really loud and they all had to line up before moving toward the Chapel. The girls were giggling at them.

It's evening now and I didn't like supper too much. It was roast pork slices or something, and I did not like the taste. I ate all the food on my plate though. All the girls are watching *Walt Disney*, but it's about an airplane and I got bored. I just finished my peanut-butter sandwich and apple juice. I'm pretending to do my homework.

I asked two girls in the bathroom if they lost their letters too, but they just looked at me and said nothing.

Monday, October 24

I woke up with a nightmare. I was dreaming that Mother and Grandma were walking away from me on the railroad track and I was yelling for them to wait for me and I ran and ran as fast as I could, but I could not get any closer and they wouldn't even turn around to wait for me!

I got up and went to the window. It was early morning and still dark. I saw a bus go by on the main street. I was just silently crying when I saw someone coming up the long wide driveway between the tall, sad-looking trees. I realized that it was the cook. I see her in the kitchen sometimes when I am sweeping the floor after breakfast. She is tall and big, has a round face, and her blond hair is always in some elastic netting over her head. She talks with a strange accent, but she just goes about her business.

Tuesday, October 25

At lunchtime, Miss Tanner called me and told me not to go back to school after I swept the dining-room floor. She's taking me to an eye doctor. She drove the Residential School car to the place. After she parked the car, she pointed to the street and I asked if I could find the building number. I was almost sure there was a little smile that quickly disappeared when she nodded. We walked down the street with the tall buildings and finally I spotted the number. We went up the steps and found the doctor's name on one of the doors.

After waiting a while, I was called into the room. The doctor asked me to cover my left eye and then my right while trying to read the letters on the wall across the room. Then a machine was placed over my face and the doctor started clicking different lenses over my eyes. After reading rows of large letters to tiny ones, I was surprised when the words on the board across the room suddenly came sharply into focus! When I was done, Miss Tanner said I could only have basic frames. They are black with a slight curve at the end. That was fine with me!

When we got back, she told me to do my homework in the dorm or take a nap if I wanted. It was too late to go back to school. She was really nice to me today.

Wednesday, October 26

We were lining up this morning, before we entered the dining room for breakfast, when Miss Tanner told us that Laura had to go home. Her little brother had an accident and had died. That was all she said. We were all shocked. We murmured our breakfast prayer and entered the dining room. Then we said the thanks prayer afterwards. No one told us what happened to the little guy.

Thursday, October 27

There is a group of four Cree girls who are always together. They don't bother anyone and I never paid much attention to them before. The leader is a girl with a pretty face. They are all from the same Reserve up north. The other three girls hover around her all the time and they even tie on her apron for her. They take off her shoes and put them on for her too. She just lifts one foot up and then the other. I hear that her father is a very important person on their Reserve. Everyone calls her Princess when she can't hear them.

It is really funny to watch. Sometimes one of the other girls will say, "Look, look, here they come," and they watch to see what Princess will do. The girls even try to do her chores for her, but they are not allowed. Miss Tanner caught them once and made Princess clean the whole washroom over again by herself.

Sunday, October 30

After lunch, one of the girls at the table was tilting her chair back and rocking it back and forth and she was making faces at another girl across the table, and I knew her chair was going to go over! Just then, she stuck out her tongue at the girl across the table and kicked her chair back and her chair went crashing down backwards! The Supervisor was on her in an instant, hauled her up and out of the dining room and straight to the office, we thought! I don't remember seeing her at supper.

Monday, October 31

It is Halloween today. I have no idea what that means.

I am ashamed to ask what Halloween is. I would really look stupid!

We made some Halloween stuff at school. Orange paper pumpkins, leaves and stuff.

I don't know why. I just have no idea what the pumpkins have to do with it. Maybe a pumpkin is *like* a Santa Claus?

We got some toffee candies wrapped in orange paper as a treat after supper.

We were just getting ready for bed when a girl screamed. We all turned to see a man's face with a horrible mask on, through the window on the fire-escape door. There is a zigzag stairway on each floor outside the building. That's where he came up from.

Next morning

We heard that the boys' two Supervisors chased the masked man off the property but did not catch him. He had disappeared into the bushes behind the building.

Thursday, November 3

I had a long cry this afternoon in the shower area. That was the only place that was empty. There are always people around and it is never quiet anywhere. Yet I feel so very alone. I haven't seen Emma in a long time. I just want to go home!

Monday, November 7

I got a letter from Grandma. I held it to my chest a long time before I pulled the page out of the envelope.

I will forever copy every letter I get from now on. I still don't know if it was the Supervisor or one of the girls who took my letters. I noticed that some of the girls got jealous if they did not get letters, and maybe it was one of them that took the letters for spite.

October 31, 1966
Dear Pynut,

It was good to hear from you. I'm glad you have good things to eat. Don't get to like television too much, because you will miss it when you get home. Yes, the storms have been really bad in the last couple of weeks. I almost got caught in a snowstorm yesterday. It was hard to see in the thick snow. I was coming back from checking my rabbit snares off the railway rock cut. The snow covered my tracks and it was hard trying to find out where I was. I had a good laugh at myself. I should have known better than to go out when I could see the clouds coming. I did find the railroad tracks, though, and I was way off down the tracks about half a mile away from where my path was! That was my adventure for the day.

I saw Blackie again when I walked by his house this morning. He has no idea what he is getting into in a story taking place very far away. I hope you bring the story home with you at Christmas. I would very much like to read it.

Now, Jennie's address is: Miss Jennie Cliennes, 17 Harrings Road, Wharton, Ontario.

She will be very happy to hear from you. I understand that she lives with her aunt.

Take care now and be happy.

> *Love always,*
> *Grandma Insy*

I was so happy that I wrote to Jennie right away, but Miss Tanner gave the letter back to me after school. "Family only," she said. Well, if I can get an envelope, I could buy a stamp to put on it. I'll have to figure that out. Maybe I can get Miss Lewis to buy me some. Maybe they have them at the corner store. I could go look sometime and see how much they cost. Yeah, that's what I'll do then, I can mail all my own letters. But, if Jennie answers back, they'll figure that out and maybe

I'll get into trouble. I don't think I'd better do that. They check all our stuff once in a while too. Miss Tanner goes through our night tables and lockers without saying when she is going to. So I'd have nowhere to hide the envelopes anyway. I keep my diary with me at all times, or between the pages of my Blackie story. At mealtimes, Miss Tanner or Miss Lewis is always present in the dining room, so no fear there.

Tuesday, November 8

After school, we were getting ready for supper when I heard my name through the intercom, saying that there was a phone call for me. I flew down the stairs and ran into the Supervisors' lounge, and just as I got there, the boys' Supervisor handed me one phone while he listened on another. Just as I picked it up, I heard Grandma say, "Is that you? Can you hear me?" in our language! Before I could answer, the Supervisor snatched the phone back and slammed it down. I could have burst into tears, but I just looked at the man in the eyes and I walked back out and up the stairs. I wanted to cry so badly, but I was halfway up the stairs when the supper bell rang, so I just ran downstairs ahead of the others. We lined up again to say our prayer before going in.

Wednesday, November 9

I think I'm going to remember the smell of food cooking every time we go up and down the stairs. That's the first thing you smell when you enter the side door.

Grandma's voice keeps repeating over and over again in my ear, "Is that you? Can you hear me?" I don't think she'll try to call again. It was so good just to hear her voice! I had a long cry again last night. I thought about her walking to the store and asking the storekeeper to put in the call for her, and then having to go home disappointed at not being allowed to talk to me. I really wish they hadn't taken my blue diary that Grandma had given me. She had written a note on the inside cover that said *To my beloved Pynut*, and I had also written some of her sayings in it. One was, "Never be louder than the little birds" when we were outside. Another was, "Let the sun see your clean and happy face first thing when it comes over the horizon" — that was so that I didn't sleep in. I'd have my face washed and hair combed and my chores done before the sun came up each morning. There were many more of her sayings that I had written in there.

I would really like to have that little diary right now.

Thursday, November 10

Everybody is coughing, sniffling and sneezing. All night, there were about three girls coughing all the time. No one got much sleep. I feel okay right now but I'll probably get a cold too. I don't feel like going to school. My head hurts.

I managed to get through the day but my throat started hurting after school. There are some empty beds. I asked the girl next to me where the girls were and she said, "In the infirmary." She laughed when I asked what on earth that was. I asked another girl what the infirmary was. She looked at me like I was stupid and said, "The sick room." Okay, so now I know. That was probably the place Miss Lewis took me to practise changing the sheets without moving me, except she never told me what the place was called.

Friday, November 11

Remembrance Day today.

We had to stand up at 11:00 at school and

stand very quiet for a whole minute. I don't quite understand what that was about. I think it has to do with a war a long time ago.

My throat still hurts and my voice sounds funny. Grandma would have picked some cedar branches and made tea from the green leaves for me to drink, and then she would have mashed the rest into a frying pan with a bit of water and flattened it all into a cheesecloth and laid it over my throat. A poultice, I think it's called in English. I better not mention that I caught a cold the next time I write to her. They might not mail my letter.

Saturday, November 12

I went into the sewing room to where a girl was sitting in front of a sewing machine. It was a different girl from the one who sewed the first booklet for me. I asked if she would sew down the middle of my new pages for me, but she just looked at me and told me to go away and that I was not supposed to be in there. More girls were coming in, so I just ran out. I'll have to figure out another way to keep my pages together for my diary.

I finished my work and it passed inspection, so I have some time this afternoon to write my Blackie story.

Monday, November 14

It is my birthday today. I am thirteen years old.

I can't talk. I have lost my voice, but otherwise, I feel okay.

The Supervisor gave me a letter from Grandma after school. It had a five-dollar bill inside for my birthday! I am going to make it last as long as I can again.

Again, I am copying this letter to my diary.

November 7th
Flint Lake
My dear Pynut.

I am thinking of you today. I want to be sure you will get this before your birthday, so I thought I would send it to you ahead of time. It has been so lonely here without you. I do miss you so. Your mother, father, brother and little sister are doing fine. I will try to call you. We have had a lot of snow this fall. Everything here is the same. Nothing new to report except that the teacher from last year did not come back. There is now a new woman teacher who everyone is grumbling about. Had a young guy bring me some wood for taking care of his sick mother. They are doing fine now.

The trains have changed schedule again so I cannot go to the small town to get some stuff and come back again. Now I have to go the other direction where I don't have to stay overnight, but it gets back quite late at night. Anyway, all that is beside the point. I am well and look forward to seeing you as soon as they let you come home. I have managed to save five dollars to send you for your birthday.

With all my love,
Grandma

I wonder what she'd say if she knew that they took my diary away. I wonder what she would have given me for my birthday if I was with her. Maybe she would have made me something.

My teardrops just blotched the writing and I brushed them away before I tucked the letter into my apron pocket.

Tuesday, November 15

I feel okay today. My voice is all right and my throat is not sore anymore.

At lunch, Miss Tanner told me that she would pick me up half an hour early from school to pick up my glasses! I am so excited!

In the afternoon, the Gym teacher took us outside. There was a long sheet of ice on the ground and he had large jam cans filled with frozen water with handles sticking up on top. They were throwing the cans to make them slide down the ice. Don't know what that was about.

Then Miss Tanner arrived and we went back to the doctor's office, and after sitting in the waiting room for a while, he called me into the small room and put the glasses on my nose, and the writing across the room was very clear! He fixed the ear curves and then I was set to go. I am so amazed at the way things are so clear! I never knew that there was anything wrong with my eyes.

I was shy when I came up to the dorm, but no one paid attention to me except the girl beside my bed. She crossed her eyes at me and stuck out her tongue at me. I laughed. After a while, I forgot about the glasses on my face.

Wednesday, November 16

Miss Lewis showed up this morning. She is filling in for Miss Tanner for a couple of days, she said. Everyone seems to relax when she is here. I think of them as Sunshine and Black Cloud. Hey, that could be another story I could write!

I'm going to write to Grandma before the supper bell rings.

November 16, 1966
Insy Pimash
Flint Lake, Ontario
Dear Grandma,

I got your letter right on my birthday, and thank you very much for the five dollars. I will make it last as long as I can. I didn't have any news to tell you, except today I have something to say. The Supervisor picked me up at King George School in the Residential School car and took me to the eye doctor yesterday. When we got there, we sat in the waiting room for a while and I was very excited. Finally the doctor called me in and he took a pair of black-framed glasses and put them on my nose. I could see very clearly all of a sudden! When we walked out of there I could see everything very clearly, even across the street with sale signs on the shop windows. I didn't know there was anything wrong with my eyes until the teacher noticed. The Supervisor then took me to see the eye doctor and I had to read tiny letters across the room and that was when he checked my eyes and found which lenses I could see from the clearest and then Miss Tanner picked out the frames for me. Now I have them on. I thought the girls and my classmates would tease and make fun of me, but no one paid any attention to me except the girl who sleeps beside me. She crossed her eyes and stuck out her tongue.

It is great to see things very clearly!

I do miss you very much and can't wait to see you again.

With all my love,
Pynut

Friday, November 18

I am feeling like I am stuck on a very long mourning period where you cannot start crying for a person who died and you have to wait for the right time. My heart and soul is starting to hurt. I can't get rid of that feeling. I just want to start crying and get out of here and go home!!! But I know I have to last until Christmas break, when they will send us all home.

I keep imagining Grandma and remembering her going about her day's schedule. I remember one time, we were walking through the path to her woodpile in the bush, when a squirrel started chirring overhead. She looked up to say something to it, and a big blob of snow landed on her face that the squirrel had knocked off from a branch. I laughed so hard I was doubled over, and she pushed me and I landed in the snow! When I walk to school, I try to remember what she would be doing that morning, and go through the whole routine with her. I walk every step with her until she gets home, safe and snug in her warm cabin. I am feeling very sad and lonely.

Saturday, November 19

Miss Lewis has this afternoon off, so she's taking me to a movie show! I don't actually know if she has told anyone. But I've never been to see a movie before, so I really don't care! We're going to take a bus to town. She mails my letters for me sometimes when she can. I managed to write a letter to Jennie and she mailed it.

We were on the bus when she handed me a letter. It was from Mother and it was not even opened! I didn't ask her how she managed to get it. I told her that she's going to get into trouble if she gets caught, but she just winked at me. I opened the letter and found a five-dollar bill. It felt so good to open the letter and know that I am the first person to read it. I always feel like I'm being cheated or (I don't know what the word is for what I feel) when I am given my letter that has already been read by someone else.

November 12, 1966
Dear Violet,

I am sending you five dollars for your birthday. Eliza is doing well and growing real fast. She and the other little boys and girls go to a little activity centre in the afternoons. She gets really excited when it's time to go and then wants to go home when we get there. Lyndon is quite a serious eight-year-old. He goes hunting with his father and checking traps with him. He is even cleaning his own kill now too. He says he is going to be a hunter, trapper and fisherman, like his father, when he grows up.

I called Grandma last week and she is doing fine. I send her some money when I can, just to help her out a bit. I don't like the new train schedule because she now has to do an overnight trip at the nearest town to get her supplies. Now she has to pay for a hotel room when she goes there.

My work is going great. I really like working at the Band Office, and I get to see all the government people who arrive on the airplane, but I also have to listen to people coming in complaining about things in the community. I am glad Izzy is not the Chief.

We have decided that we will all go to Grandma's place to see you when you come home for Christmas. It would be too hard for you to come here, too, after getting off the train at Grandma's. We can't wait to see you.

Take care of yourself.

Your Mother,
Emily

I put the letter into my pocket and was quiet for a while until Miss Lewis asked if everything was okay. I smiled and thanked her again.

I really liked the movie and I got to taste theatre popcorn for the first time, and the pop was good too. The movie was about a little boy and his dog. It gave me some ideas for Blackie's adventures. I was starting to run out of things for Blackie to get into. Maybe that's why Miss Lewis decided to take me. I don't know. I didn't ask her. I kept thanking her over and over again for taking me, until she burst out laughing and said, "Enough, enough!"

I asked her what her first name was on the way home and she said "Jo" and I smiled and asked her, "Like in a boy's name, 'Joe'?" She laughed and said "No, 'Jo.' That is short for Josephine. But, don't forget, you are not to call me by my first name when I'm at work." I won't forget.

Sunday, November 20

Emma finally came this afternoon, but with a boy. I was so disappointed. I wanted to talk to her about going home for Christmas, and I didn't like the pimple-faced dark boy. His name sounded very different and he kept frowning at me like I was in the way. We went to the park and after a while I realized that they were spending the whole time talking to each other and I was just following them. Finally, I just said that I had to get back and finish my homework. I ran all the way back.

Monday, November 21

I took a shortcut to the corner store about two blocks from the Residential School after school. When I came out, I was unwrapping the chocolate bar when I heard a shout, "There's one!"

I saw five teenaged white boys running across the street and I looked around me and that's when I realized they were running toward me! I just took off as fast as I could. I raced to the main road and down the street, but I could still hear them behind me. I came around the corner and ran across the road and just barely missed being hit by a car. It screeched to a halt and I heard a man yelling. I glanced back and the man was getting out of the car and shouting at the boys. I had a stitch in my side so I slowed down when I saw the tree-lined driveway to the Residential School. The boys were no longer behind me. I walked up the driveway and sat down on the first of the wide steps and slowly ate my chocolate bar.

I wonder what they would have done to me if they had caught me. I have to watch out for them.

Wednesday, November 23

I got home from school and I could tell that someone had gone through my things. The things in my night-table drawer were moved around. I always put my letters in the order that I get them, and they were all mixed up. But at least they were still there! The things in my locker were also moved around. I don't like it when people touch my stuff! I wish I had a place where I can hide my things. My desk at school isn't mine either. Other students sit there when we move classes.

Although I write in very tiny letters, my diary is getting thick. I have three of the booklets now and I don't know where to hide them. Right now, they are in between the pages of my Blackie story.

Saturday, November 26

I just spent the last of the five dollars from Grandma. I bought a sponge toffee at the little shop at the park. I still have Mother's five dollars though.

Emma came to visit me this afternoon. She said she felt bad about Sunday. Her boyfriend had to go out of town with his family this weekend, and so we spent the time at the park. She had some money from her father. She still seems to be happy in the home that she lives at. The people are very nice, she says. It was good to see her and I asked when we would be going home for Christmas. She says it will probably be the week before the 22nd of December. I can't wait!

Monday, November 28

I am waiting for the breakfast bell to ring.

I have not answered Mother's letter yet. I don't have anything to say.

After school I got a letter from Grandma! I have copied it here.

November 20, 1966
Dear Pynut,

I hope you are well and happy. I am coming along fine and I look forward to seeing you real soon. It is only one month away now. I took the train to Sandy Bay last week. I was at a church rummage sale — that's the big church they have there — and I met an older Anishinabe woman, like me. We got to talking and we left the church at the same time, so we decided to go into the restaurant and have a cup of tea. Well, she invited me to come to her house. She lives alone and only her son comes to check up on her sometimes, and to fix things that need fixing. Anyway, she invited me to stay with her every time I come into town. She has a nice little house and since I had not gone to the hotel yet, I accepted her offer and I stayed there overnight. She has an extra room that

her son sleeps in when he comes. She had a pot
of beef stew simmering on the stove when we
got there, and fresh bannock on the table. We
sat up talking and drinking tea at the kitchen
table late into the night. I really enjoyed that.
I had never had so much tea!

I am going to have a special treat for you
when you get home. I will make you a feast
that you will never forget! I am busy making
moccasins for the storekeeper and his family.
He even paid me half ahead of time. He says
he'll pay me the rest when he gets them. That
was nice of him, since I will have to buy more
thread, needles and beads.

It is snowing again outside. It is really
pretty, but it is hard walking through the snow.
I don't worry though. I have a big stack of wood
and I am cozy warm.

Write again soon, Pynut. I really miss you.

Love,

Grandma

Thursday, December 1

I decided to write a letter to Mother before the
supper bell rings. I have no homework right now.
I really hope she is getting my letters.

December 1, 1966

Dear Mother,

I just got a letter from Grandma and she has found a friend at Sandy Bay and she doesn't have to get a hotel room anymore. Her friend has a little house that she can stay at.

Sorry that I have not written earlier. I have nothing to write about. I'm doing all right and I look forward to seeing you all at Grandma's at Christmas. Where will we all sleep in Grandma's little cabin? Some people will have to sleep on the floor between the two single beds. That will be fun!

I have a pair of glasses now. They have a black frame and they are curved a bit at the corners. I can see really clear now. I didn't know that there was anything wrong with my eyes. I also got a filling in my back left tooth. It didn't hurt at all.

It's hard to believe that it is actually December now. I can't wait to get home.

Write again soon.

Your daughter,
Violet

The bell just rang and we have to line up.

Friday, December 2

I went with an older girl to babysit on the next street. Her name is Helen. We walked through the woods to get there.

The blond woman was nice. She has two children, a boy about four and a little girl about two years old. I was telling her about the paper dolls we used to play at home that we cut out from an old Eaton's catalogue. She ran downstairs to her basement and came up with an old Eaton's catalogue and she gave it to me to cut up when we get back to the Residential School. I was so grateful!

Saturday, December 3

Someone noticed that Princess was missing from our lineup for breakfast. The three girls do not know where she has gone or when she had left. They were crying in the lineup and Miss Tanner had to take them away.

Sunday, December 4

There's still no sign of Princess. Everyone is whispering ideas and suggestions, but no one knows, and Miss Tanner won't say, either. One older girl said that they probably sent her to another Residential School. I don't understand any of this.

Monday, December 5

After supper, my two friends Sarah and Mary decided to ask if we can go upstairs to the storage room to cut up the Eaton's catalogue. Miss Lewis is on duty for a couple of days because Miss Tanner had to go somewhere. She gave us a pair of paper scissors and we sneaked up to the third storage floor and we sat down beneath the window and cut out our paper dolls. We had a lot of fun!

When we were ready to leave, Mary told us that this is her second year here and that two of her sisters had stayed here too, but that this third floor was where the little ones used to stay. It was called the Junior Dorm then. The older girls on the second floor could hear their little sisters crying up here, but they were not allowed to come up to comfort them. That sounded very sad.

Tuesday, December 6

I really enjoyed supper. It was some kind of hamburger and macaroni casserole with lots of cheese on top. Some of the girls always complain of tummy aches every time we have cheese in our meals. Or some, even when they have a glass of milk at night. I don't know why. I can eat anything, it seems. It doesn't bother me.

Nothing much to write about.

Wednesday, December 7

I noticed one of the girls on a park bench on the way home from school. I went to her because I could tell she was crying. Her name is Wendy. She is from a Reserve next to the one where Mother lives. I asked her what was wrong and she told me that she got a letter yesterday saying that her mother got married. I asked her how that was bad. She said her father just died last year and she has two small brothers and a baby sister. When I asked if she knew the man her mother married, she nodded her head. She said that his wife died two years ago and that he has four children. They are all under ten. That's a lot of children, I am thinking. But he has no wife to look after his children and she had no husband to look after her and her children. I told Wendy that her mother would need someone to look after and take care of her and her children. I asked her if the man was a bad man or violent. She shook her head.

So I asked her why she was crying. She got mad and said, "You don't understand anything!" and ran off.

I guess I don't.

Thursday, December 8

Miss Tanner took a look at my chest when I was taking off my apron and she said, "Come with me." I followed her upstairs and she opened a door and there were rows and rows of shelves. She walked along and then stopped and pulled out a stack of bras. She glanced at me and pulled down two of the bras and put down my number on them and told me to put one on. I looked at it, trying to figure out which way the clips were supposed to go, and then she sighed, pulled open my blouse and showed me how to put it on, and then I was back downstairs again. I looked down at my small tits poking out beneath my shirt and I got very shy. I didn't want anyone to see my newly pointed tits!

Nobody paid any attention to me at all!

Friday, December 9

The Gym teacher had us sit on the floor and he got us to stretch our legs apart and stretch out and reach as far as we could on the floor. I did not like this at all! It seemed very — well, girls just don't do that! You never, ever, spread your legs out like that. So, I pretended to hurt my side. I don't mind the running around or playing ball. I'm still trying to get used to the bra. It feels like something pressing my ribs in, and my shoulders are sore from the straps too.

Saturday, December 10

The Cree girls must have found our paper dolls. Everything is gone!

Sarah started crying, but Mary said that it was probably not the Cree girls. She said that maybe Miss Lewis told "the others" about the paper dolls and maybe they told her to get rid of the dolls and the catalogue because we would be playing about home and having our dolls talk in our language. I think so too.

I told them that we would talk about home instead. Sarah said that she was glad to have left home. She said her mother was never home and they were hungry most of the time. She has a little sister and brother there. It was sad to hear her story.

Mary came from a big family, but her brothers and sisters had already left home. She says she really loves spending all her time at home with her parents, and they always go somewhere camping when she gets home.

I remember her telling us that her two sisters were at this school too. She said they are married now and had to move to their husbands' Reserves, and her brothers are working at an airport of some kind.

I told them about Grandma and Mother. We spent all afternoon there until the bell rang for supper. We had to scramble fast down the stairs in order to line up in time before the Supervisor came. Then we all marched down the stairs and lined up before the dining room again to say the prayer there before we go inside. After the meal, there's that prayer to say and then we get up and clean the dining room. It is getting so that I don't even think about what I am saying at prayers anymore. We just all speak and say the same thing together.

Monday, December 12

My letters are gone again! I thought I was going to explode — I was so mad!!! I've calmed down a bit now. Everyone is just going about their business and no one's paying any attention to me. I never see anyone upset either. I see the other girls get mail, and they put the letters in their lockers, but I never hear anyone say that they are gone. I feel ready to burst into tears, but I will not cry!

It's after school and I don't have any homework. I'm just going to write this until the supper bell rings.

I've been thinking about Wendy. I think I finally figured out why she was so upset.

She thinks that her father has been replaced and her mother is now with another man. That got me thinking about Grandma. I remember asking her about my grandfather. We were sitting along the shoreline cooling off after picking blueberries along the railway tracks. I am thinking it is important for me to write this down so that I can read it when I am feeling really lost and stripped down. Grandma seems too much a part of me to lose. I want to feel her alive with me every day.

She said that her family lived up north at her father's trapline. One winter they came into the village to pick up some groceries and supplies. They were at the store when a young man walked in. He was the son of another trapper, and when he saw her, his face lit up. He walked toward Grandma's father to say hello, but he was so close that he stepped on one of Grandma's moccasins and she lost her balance when she tried to step back and landed flat on her bottom! They were married that summer when she was nineteen years old, and then a year later, Mother was born. Mother was five years old when the Government plane landed at the trapline and took her away, under threat that my grandparents would be thrown in prison and would never see their child again if they didn't let her go. Grandma was thirty-four years old when Grandpa fell through the ice and drowned. She never remarried. She looked after her parents until they were gone. All those years while Mother was at Residential School, Grandma lived in the cabin by herself and hunted and fished to keep herself alive. And then I came along. For a long time there were just the three of us. I don't remember much of that though. Then Mother married Izzy. That was when we had to move away from Grandma, and Izzy took us up north to his Reserve. I remember that I wasn't very happy.

Now, here I am. I won't forget who I am.

Tuesday, December 13

I don't know where the information came from or if it's just gossip, but someone said that Princess had made it home. I don't know. I hope she did. I often wondered how she made it out of the building without anyone seeing her. She must have had some money to be able to get away like that. I wouldn't know the first thing to do to get out of here. I'd have to make it to the train station and buy a ticket, and then to where? I can't even remember the place where we had to spend the night. I bet the train ticket agent would be on the phone to the Residential School the minute I showed up!

I've also noticed that Princess's three Cree girls aren't even speaking to each other now. Maybe they feel mad at being left here. Who knows!

Thursday, December 15

Countdown to going home! Six more days!

We had a pork chop each with mashed potatoes and peas for supper.

There's a high excited feeling in the dorm. I don't know how to describe it. It's like everyone is waiting for something to happen. Some of the girls began running around and chasing each other up and down the stairs when I heard a man's voice bellow from down below. That must be the boys' Supervisor. Their lounge room is across the double doors to the stairway.

It's very quiet in the dorm right now. I don't feel like writing anymore. I keep thinking about Grandma. I can't wait to see her.

Friday, December 16

Five more days until I see Grandma!

Everyone in my class at King George is talking about Christmas. They are mostly talking about the presents they are hoping to get and what they have asked their parents for. Also the decorations that they are putting up inside and outside their homes. There are also shiny decorations hanging along the hallway and at the school office window. Everyone seems happier than normal. I just don't understand what the excitement is about. I also don't really understand who this Santa Claus is and why he is so important. I know that there are usually boxes of toys that are sent to the Reserve. They are given out to the kids at the school at Christmas, but there is really no mention of Santa Claus that I can remember. Maybe he really is something like the Halloween pumpkin.

Saturday, December 17

Four more days until I see Grandma!

There are all kinds of Christmas shows on television too. Wendy, Mary and I went downtown this afternoon and there are Christmas decorations on the store windows and everything is glittering and shiny! It was really pretty. We just walked up and down the street looking at the window displays. Then we had to run back in a hurry because we forgot to look at the time. We just got in the door and kicked off our shoes and hung up our jackets and were barely in time to line up for supper outside the dining room.

Sunday, December 18

Three more days until I see Grandma!

We will be walking along the path back to her cabin. We will pass by Blackie's cabin too. I wonder if he will come out to greet us? It will be nice to see him too.

If the snow is very deep, Grandma makes a path to the train tracks from her cabin because the train tracks are always clear of snow. We'll probably sit with the lamp on and talk for a while before bed — me from my single bed beside the window and her from her bed at the other corner of the room. She'll have the stove going nice and warm too.

Can't wait to get home!

Tuesday, December 20

There was an announcement over the intercom.

Our trips home have been cancelled!

One of the girls has developed German measles and we are quarantined! I don't even know who the girl is. She is in the infirmary under quarantine. I really wasn't sure what quarantine meant, so I asked one of the girls.

I can't stop crying. Everyone is red eyed.

The girls are saying that if we go home, we might carry the sickness home, where some pregnant woman will lose her baby. *I* don't know any pregnant women back home! I want to go home!!!

Wednesday, December 21

We were supposed to be going home today!

I cried a long time last night. I feel so cheated!

I wasn't the only one either. All night in the pitch-blackness, I kept hearing sniffles and silent screams. Someone actually screamed into her pillow. It was awful!

Thursday, December 22

There was one girl who seemed very happy. She was laughing and chatting when she had always been quiet. She was even getting very angry as it came close to going home too. She was laughing at me when she noticed that I had been crying when I came out of the toilet stall. "What are you laughing at? Why aren't you sad?" I asked her as I bent to wash my face. There were just the two of us in the bathroom. She said, "I am not going home, that's why! I get to avoid Christmas at home this year. People kill each other at Christmas where I come from. We are always so scared. I had to hide under the bed with my two little sisters for almost a whole day last year. It's just so . . ." Then she just turned and said "Never mind!" and went out the door.

I've heard that in some places there is a lot of alcohol and violence during the holidays. That must be what she means.

Friday, December 23

There is a concert for us tonight. The local Anishinabe high-school boys have a band and they are going to come and play for us!

We had to line up as usual before we entered

a large room that I had never seen before. It was right across from the Principal's office, I think.

Later

Well, we just got back and no time to watch television. The kitchen girls just brought us our evening snack of a slice of cake each and hot chocolate, and we just sat around the floor and talked about the concert. We don't usually have cake, so this is a nice treat. Chocolate cake with thick icing on top!

The concert was in a large room that they called an auditorium, with a stage of some sort at front. The guys were up on a floor about 4 feet higher than us. They had guitars and drums and one guy sang at the front. The four guys sang some songs and I did recognize some Beatles songs from the time that I was home on the Reserve when the radio was on, and then here on the television. Some other songs I had not heard before.

Oh, well. I think I would have preferred to watch television.

Saturday, December 24

Nothing happening today. I didn't feel like going anywhere, so I thought I'd write to Grandma.

There isn't even anything to write about. I gave up on that idea. I don't even feel like writing my Blackie story either. I keep wanting to end the story, but then I think of something else Blackie could get into. I am just going to leave it for now.

My sketch of Grandma's cabin is finished. I just added myself walking beside Grandma. I am carrying a bag of potatoes!

Sunday, December 25

We had to pin the little doily things to our heads again this morning. Then we trudged through the bush in deep snow to get to the Church for the Christmas service. Same thing. The man up front was talking and talking, and I watched the people bobbing up and down the whole time. Maybe it kept their legs from falling asleep. I want to go home!!!

Monday, December 26

Today is Boxing Day. Don't know what that means either. The only "boxing" I have ever heard of are the guys that punch each other until one of them falls down and can't get up again.

A girl was crying in the bathroom this morning. Someone put a wad of gum in her hair while she was sleeping and Miss Lewis had to cut it out. Now she has a bald spot on the side of her head! I felt sorry for her. Whoever did it would not tell.

Some of the girls were saying after breakfast that she probably had the gum in her mouth when she went to sleep and it fell out of her mouth and got into her hair during the night when she'd be moving around. Oh, well. They call her Bald Spot now.

Tuesday, December 27

After supper, they took us to the hockey rink downtown to see a hockey game. We travelled by bus. The boys were in it too and we were supervised by the boys' Supervisor and our own Miss Lewis. I didn't know anything about hockey and soon got bored watching guys skating around shooting a flat black round thing back and forth.

Saturday, December 31

Today is New Year's Eve.

I just remembered last year at Flint Lake with Grandma. It was right after midnight and I started hearing gunshots being fired into the air. I remember wondering how many bullets rained down on the community that night. After all, what goes up must come down.

Sunday, January 1, 1967

Today is New Year's Day.

It would be "hugs and kisses" day today at Flint Lake. I wonder who would come up the trail to give Grandma a hug and a kiss, now that Ol' Moses is gone. I remember Grandma making faces at me over his shoulder when he gave her a hug and a kiss. He made a funny hissing noise when he laughed.

I never had to explain to Grandma that I was very uncomfortable with people hugging me because Mother never did. I don't ever remember one hug from my mother. Grandma hugs me sometimes, though, like when I haven't seen her for a long time.

Grandma explained to me once that Mother went to Residential School far away to the west. They took her away when Mother was only five years old, and there was nothing Grandma could do about it. It was very bad in the Residential School where Mother went. They were not allowed to hug, and she was pushed away if she got hurt and ran to someone for help. They got hit all the time by the Supervisors and their food was not very good and they were always hungry. They were treated very badly and it would break Grandma's heart when Mother told her all that happened when she got home each year. It must have been a horrible feeling.

Oh, I'm really, really going to get into trouble if they see this entry.

Monday, January 2

I'm on bathroom-cleaning duty this month, along with another girl. We are wiping down the counter with the three mirrors on the wall above it. Wiping the round sink. Wiping the windows and the walls. Wiping down the toilet stalls. Scrubbing the toilet bowls and mopping the floor. We take turns. We have to work fast and do a good job. The Supervisor comes to inspect the work until she finds nothing to complain about.

Tuesday, January 10

I haven't written anything for a whole week. Don't feel like it. Nothing to say.

Going back to school was really sad yesterday. The girls are very quiet in the dorm most of the time, since Christmas. Everybody seems to be lying around on their beds every chance they get. No one feels like doing anything. There are no more fights and arguments anymore either.

After supper

Bald Spot went into a fit. I think her name is Dorothy — she never really talked much to anyone before. She started screaming in the toilet stall and wouldn't come out. Miss Tanner and the boys' Supervisor had to come and open the door to take her out and we never saw her again. We have no idea what happened to her. Everyone shuts up and there is nothing you can get out of anyone. I even asked Miss Tanner where the girl was but she just looked at me and walked away.

Wednesday, January 11

I have nothing worth writing about. I don't even feel like writing to Grandma. I have nothing to say. I just wish I was home. It's a horrible feeling when I want something so much but I can't have it and there's nothing I can do about it.

Still no word about Bald Spot.

Friday, January 13

I tried to write something in my Blackie story, but after a while, I gave up. I just don't feel like writing anything anymore.

Saturday, January 14

After lunch, Helen came up to me and asked if I wanted to go with her to babysit. I was glad to get out of the place, so I went. We trudged up the path to the Chapel and down to the street. The blond woman asked me about the catalogue that she had given me and I told her we had a lot of fun making paper dolls, and thanked her again. I didn't say what happened to it. We played with the children in the living room until the woman came home. This time Helen gave me a dollar from the money that the woman gave her. That was a nice afternoon. We had fun.

Sunday, January 15

Emma came to visit me. We sat in the large room by the door, just leaning against the wall, and she told me about her trip home at Christmastime. Her brothers and sisters had been complaining about their new teacher. But she said that she just got a letter from Mike to say that the bad teacher never came back after Christmas. They have a new teacher and he is a very nice young man. The kids are happy again.

I told her about our miserable Christmas here. I asked about her boyfriend — he goes to the same high school as Emma — and she said that she does not see him anymore. They happened to run into his sister on the street downtown, and next thing, he wouldn't talk to her anymore. I was kind of glad about that. I didn't like him anyway.

Monday, January 16

I almost panicked on my way home. I had been talking to myself in Anishinabe so that I wouldn't forget the language, and I was naming the things I was seeing and I was watching the small icy balls of snow coming down, and then I couldn't remember what that kind of snow is called! It was driving me crazy, so when I got to the dorm, I whispered the question to a girl who was standing by the window, but she just turned and looked at me in a weird way and walked away. Maybe she just realized that she didn't remember it either. I'll probably remember it sooner or later.

Tuesday, January 17

A group of white boys chased me back to the Residential School again. I was busy talking to myself and had my head down, watching my feet come into view one after the other, when I heard a shout. They were laughing and giggling, coming toward me in a flat-out run, so I took off. First I thought they were just crossing the road, but then I realized they were chasing me. I was a good runner at home, running along the railway tracks. I ran for 3 whole miles without stopping one time. So these guys didn't last long before I left them behind.

Wednesday, January 18

I got a letter from Grandma! I was just coming into the dorm when I heard Miss Tanner call my name and she handed me the envelope. I don't care now if it is opened and read before I get it. I am just so happy Grandma wrote!

Flint Lake
January 11, 1967
Dear Pynut,
I have not heard from you in a long time. I hope you are doing fine. We had a very cold

spell for about a week and we also got a nasty snowstorm. The high winds put up high snow drifts and it totally wiped out my path to the store. Young Rob — that young man and his wife who had the baby last spring — came up with two full pails of water, and he split and brought in more wood for me. That was so nice of him. I was beginning to wonder if I would be forced to melt some snow for water. Rob also made a path for me down to the lake and even opened up my water hole for me. He also cleared my path to the railroad tracks so that I could make it to the store. I must think of something I could do for them. Maybe I can buy some fabric from the rummage sale at Sandy Bay where my friend lives. I stay with her when I go there. She is always so glad of the company. If I get enough fabric, I think I will make that young family a really nice quilt. They would like that.

Do write back and let me know how you are getting on. Remember what I told you the last time I saw you. I miss you and look forward to hearing from you soon.

Love,
Grandma

I had to put my head down and wipe my eyes before anyone saw me. I made it to the washroom before I could have a good cry. I washed my face after, and then the bell rang for supper. I will write back tomorrow.

Thursday, January 19

I have been thinking about that line about me remembering what Grandma said to me the last time I saw her, at the train station. She put a hand on my head and over my chest and said for me to be a good girl and be strong. How do I be strong in my head and in my heart? Maybe I have to think good thoughts and ask my heart not to be so sad. How do I tell her that?

January 19, 1967
Insy Pimash
Flint Lake, Ontario
Dear Grandma,

I was so happy to get your letter yesterday. I have been thinking about what you said and I think I understand. I will work harder at school and do the best I can and be as happy as I can. I am going to start writing my Blackie story again. I kind of left it since before Christmas, but I still have it with my homework papers. I will read it to you when I get home. Maybe I will start by drawing a picture of Blackie for the cover first.

We get a snack with a glass of milk in the evening while we watch television. Last night it was peanut-butter-and-jam sandwiches. Two girls make them in the kitchen downstairs and they bring them up on a large tray. Then they take the empty glasses back down when we are done.

That sounds like a really bad storm you had. We get snowy, windy days here too, but I don't think they are as bad as where you are. That was nice of Rob to help you out. I never really visited anyone when I was there. I should go and visit his wife and baby the next time I get home. Emma still visits me once in a while. She told me all about her trip back home at Christmas. I imagine you going about your daily chores and sitting down sewing by the table to get the better light from the window. You must have finished those moccasins for the storekeeper's family already. I miss you too.

Stay safe and write again soon.

Love,
Pynut

Sunday, January 22

I seem to have memorized the words to some of the hymns that we sing at the Chapel. I really like singing together with the others. I forget myself sometimes and then I get self-conscious when I realize that my voice is clearer and louder than the others and I suddenly tune it down and hunch up my shoulders! I hope no one has noticed.

Monday, January 23

I had my first real understanding of the English words "piece" and "peace."

I never had to use the word "peace" in all my writing, so I had never noticed it.

I should also mention that I am still having problems pronouncing "soap" and "soup." Why is it "goose" and "geese" and "moose" but not "meese"? The English language is %#*@#! I discovered those symbols in a superhero comic that showed up and disappeared in the dorm so quickly, like a snowflake that just blew in! I don't know who brought it in or who took it away.

Thursday, January 26

It has taken me this long, but I think I am beginning to understand that there is no rhyme or reason to the spelling of the English language. I just have to memorize the spelling and not worry about trying to understand the rules. I got all correct answers on the spelling test today!

Friday, January 27

I learned there are many words that are spelled the same way but they mean many different things. "Butt" can be animals butting things with their heads, the butt end of a weapon or tool, a cigarette butt and being the butt of a joke. Then there is "their," "there" and "they're." They are easier to remember, but then there's "cite," "sight" and "site." I didn't know anything about "cite" so I had to look it up. I am sure there are many words like that. I don't know. I find it all very confusing!

I got a letter from Mother when we got home after school. I haven't heard from her in a long time. I have to copy it right away when I finish reading it, in case it disappears tomorrow.

January 19, 1967
Dear Violet,

I hope you are doing fine and learning a lot from your school. There must be many different things you are learning there than you would have over here. Tell me all about it when you get home.

Grandma had a bad cold last week but she seems to be okay now. I talked to the storekeeper when he told me that she would not likely be coming to the store any time soon, but there's a young man who looks in on her to make sure she has what she needs.

Everyone is doing well here. The kids are all healthy, but Izzy got into an accident at the Band Office. He came to pick up Eliza because I had to work late, and just as they were going out the door, Eliza slipped and he went to grab her and then he slipped and fell down the stairs. His ankle swelled really badly, but he did not break it. It was a really bad sprain though. He had to hop around on crutches for about a week.

I haven't heard from you in a long time and I was just so sorry and sad that you could not come home for Christmas. You will be home soon though. Just do the best you can and be a good girl and do as you are told and you'll be fine.

Write back soon and let me know how you are.

Your Mother,
Emily

Well, I'll have to think of something to say, because right now, I don't know what to write about. Funny that she doesn't say anything about my glasses that I told her about in my last letter. Maybe they never even mailed it.

I have to do my homework before the supper bell rings.

Saturday, January 28

I should write back to my mother, but I can't think of anything to say.

Sunday, January 29

We went to the Chapel again this morning and I really belted out some hymns this morning and I didn't care who heard me. I felt such a shock hit the top of my head during the chorus and the shock travelled clear down to my toes. The girls beside me turned and smiled at me and they sang louder too! That was a lot of fun!

In between the hymns, we sit and listen to the Principal talking. Actually, I was thinking about Flint Lake and the Indian Day School there. The government built the schools so that the kids didn't have to be sent to Residential School until they reach Grade 5. There was no instruction on Church and the Bible. The teachers were hired by Indian Affairs. There were no religious topics at the Reserve school either, that I can remember. So I don't know very much about what the words mean in the hymns. Or the prayers we have to say.

Tuesday, January 31

I decided to write back to Mother. I don't have any homework today.

January 31, 1967
Dear Mother,

Another month is gone. Soon it will be spring and then summer.

I really enjoy the art classes at school. We did something called a papier mâché and we pasted pieces of paper soaked in glue with different colours and different writing on it, and we made animals and things with it. It was fun but mucky. Sometimes we get to draw anything we like. I decided to draw a black dog called Blackie from Flint Lake. I am writing a story about him and I am making the book cover for it. I had to do it over and over again though. I did not know it was so hard to sketch a dog's face. The first one looked really scary! It looked like a big human face with lots of hair on it and its ears really looked like horns. I asked Teacher how I could go about drawing a dog's face. He told me to try the eyes and nose first. It still looked like a scary face. So, I decided to draw it from sideways. Now I have a good snout and his head and ears look good. He looks like a dog, but then I ran into trouble with the eye. The first eye I drew looked like a big human eye glued to the side of his head! I'll figure it out. If I could find a picture of a dog with his head sideways, then I can just work from that.

Sorry about going on about Blackie. I am doing fine and working hard at school. I look forward to the television shows that we get to watch in the evenings.

Say hello to Eliza, Lyndon and Izzy for me.
Write again soon.

Your daughter,
Violet

Thursday, February 2

Today is Groundhog Day. I decided to ask my English teacher what that meant.

Now this is really very puzzling to me. What's a groundhog doing telling people if it is going to be springtime now or later? Stupid people! Poor groundhog probably doesn't even know what's going on. He should be sleeping.

I am back on duty polishing the wax on the dorm floor again and sweeping up the dining room after meals.

Thursday, February 9

After school, I was running up the stairs and one of the girls tripped me. I fell down onto the landing and my papers went flying just as Miss Tanner was coming out of the dorm. I almost panicked when I saw my diaries slide out of my story, but she was busy looking at the girl who had tripped me and I had time to grab them and slip them into my notebooks. Miss Tanner didn't even look at me or say anything, except to crook a finger at the girl and they went off to the office. That was too close!!!

We had to walk in the blizzard all the way to school this morning. It was cold! The snow stopped by the time school was over, but there were very high snowdrifts. I ran most of the way back. I passed the boys from the Residential School and they did not like me running by them, so they ran with me all the way back. I laughed when a boy ran right beside me for quite a while with a big grin on his face. We soon left the others behind us. He kept glancing at me. I think his name is David. He's one of the Cree boys. He is on sweeping duty in the dining room too, on the boys' side after meals.

Saturday, February 11

Miss Lewis is gone. I guess she got the Nurse's job that she had applied for. I miss her.

We have a new weekend Supervisor named Miss Scott. She has short blond curly hair and bright blue eyes. Some of the other girls knew her from last year and they were very quiet when she came in. She seems nice. She told us new girls that she was here last year, but got another weekend job in the fall, so she is back with us for the winter term.

At least this one smiles. Miss Tanner still never smiles and never says very much.

Oh, she would get mad if she saw this entry! I could honestly get caught one day.

Sunday, February 12

We went to the Chapel again this morning and this time almost half of the girls were singing! We were all singing at the top of our voices, especially at the chorus! I wish they would let us choose some of the hymns ourselves. Some of them are pretty boring, but there are some that are really nice to sing together to.

Monday, February 13

David and I raced home again today. We left everyone behind again! That was really nice. I don't see him sweep the dining-room floor anymore. He must be doing some other chore. I don't ever talk to him. We just run. When we get here he runs on to the boys' door and I run to ours.

Tuesday, February 14

Today is Valentine's Day.

We got to make Valentine's cards at school and it was rather embarrassing. One of the white boys in the class put one on my desk with his name on it. I got very shy and couldn't think of a thing to say. I made a pretty one for Grandma. I'll send it to her the next time I write. I'll see if they mail it.

Wednesday, February 15

I got a letter from Mother this afternoon.

February 6, 1967
Dear Violet,

I just had to write a letter to tell you that Izzy killed a moose on Friday afternoon. We decided to go and camp for the weekend where he had killed it and we roasted and dried the meat over an open fire. The couple next door came with us and we really had a lot of fun.

We set up two canvas tents face to face and built a tarp over the top of both tents so that it formed a porch. There's a small wood stove in each tent and we piled the split wood in the makeshift porch. That's where we stacked the sheets of dried moose meat after we had cooked and smoked it. Your brother and sister had a lot of fun. We ate and laughed as we worked.

Your brother has a puppy that he will train as a hunting dog. He is a male and is black and white and he is about five months old. He kept everyone laughing with all his tricks.

Lyndon is very happy in the bush. He will make a good hunter and trapper when he grows up, which is all he has ever wanted to do.

Eliza is also very happy. She is growing very fast and she was a big help keeping the fire going and getting more spruce branches for us to sit on while we worked around the fire with the meat.

Now, it is back to work and I am sending this letter out in the afternoon mail flight. I hope all is well with you. Take care of yourself and write back soon.

Your Mother,
Emily

I am glad someone is having fun. I don't know what to feel about this. I am happy they had fun. I don't know what I should say when I answer this letter.

I guess I'll think of something. The supper bell is going to ring soon.

Thursday, February 16

I decided to try to send Grandma the Valentine's card I made. I don't know if they'll send it. I didn't have time to write anything yesterday. We had to stand in line for a very long time before supper. Finally, Miss Tanner allowed us to sit on the floor while she went into the kitchen. We could hear the boys' Supervisor laughing hard at something. Miss Tanner came back with her straight face and didn't say anything. Finally, we were told to stand up again and we said our prayer before going into the dining room. We never found out what the problem was. Some of the girls were joking that maybe the cook fell asleep and had to start cooking our supper just when the supper bell rang!

I still don't know how to answer Mother's letter.

I decided to write to Grandma instead and I dated it from Tuesday when it was actually Valentine's Day.

February 14, 1967
Insy Pimash
Flint Lake, Ontario
Dear Grandma,

I had a really nice day today. We made Valentine's cards in Art class today and I decided to make you one. There is a white boy in class who is always very nice to me. He would hand over a pencil if I couldn't find mine, or he would tell me the page number that the teacher was talking about in the textbook if I missed it. That really helps. It makes me feel like I am not so very alone. So, when we finished with the Valentine's cards, I had made this one for you and the boy came over and put the one he had made on my desk! I didn't know what to do, so I just whispered "thanks." It seems people exchange cards with big hearts and love signs here on Valentine's Day. I don't know what "Valentine" actually means — don't know who or what it is — could be a person or a fairy. I suppose, Valentine could also be a guy like Cupid.

Anyway, hope things are going all right with you. Is the weather beginning to warm up yet? I have been seeing birds that are much too early for spring here, but trees and birds are all different here. I am keeping my spirits up and doing the best I can to find things to do that make me happy. I have picked up my story about Blackie again. I didn't know it was going to be so hard when I first thought up that project!

I got a letter from Mother about Izzy killing a moose and how much fun they had camping out in the snow to work on the meat. I am still thinking about how I should answer that letter. I don't know anything about that stuff. The last time Izzy killed a moose when I was there, he just got some other guys in the community to go with him to get the meat and he brought a chunk home. I guess I'll think of something.

Write again soon, Grandma. I really miss you.

Love,

Pynut

Friday, February 17

I've decided to write down the names of things so I don't forget them. That way, I can read them before I write down the things for my diary. Grandma will think it's funny.

I had a nightmare where I saw Grandma and

I couldn't remember any Anishinabe words to tell her what I wanted to say. It was like I had no mouth, and she would just look at me and wait to hear what I have to say and I struggle to say something. I was crying when I woke up. I think it's because sometimes I can't remember what a thing is called in Anishinabe when I see it.

robin — *opichina*

aandeg — crow

papaasae — red-headed woodpecker

kwikwishi — Canada jay

I am not sure if there is a proper spelling for these names, so I am putting them down what they sound like.

mooningwanae — flicker (I had to look up what this bird is called in English at the King George School library)

goose — *nika*

loon — *maang*

mallard — *aninishib*

owl — *kookooko'oo*

grouse — *pinae*

seagull — *kuyaashk*

Oops, the supper bell just rang.

Saturday, February 18

I saw David sweeping the boys' side of the dining room this morning. He smiled at me as I was sweeping the girls' side. Then he pushed his pile of dust onto my side just as I saw the boys' Supervisor come around the corner behind him. He saw David and he yelled at him to pick up his own dust. I giggled. David got caught!

Sunday, February 19

We just went to the Chapel today and are doing nothing much again today.

We had another really nice singalong with one hymn, but the rest were really sad and boring. I don't understand why the Principal thinks he has to talk on and on about nothing really. Most of the time I tune out, as I have no idea what he is talking about.

Emma has not visited me in a while. I have no idea what she's doing.

I'm feeling really bad. I'm having really bad dreams. Last night I dreamt that I was running in the bush, trying to get home, but didn't know which way to go and something was chasing me. I can't really think clear or concentrate on home-work or I find myself looking outside the window at school when the teacher is talking. I just want to go home!!!

I started imagining today that if I got an early start one day, I could probably walk to the train station and use the few dollars that I have managed to save, and maybe I could get away. But I know I don't have enough money even to get me to the next town.

I just cry myself to sleep. There is nothing else to do.

Monday, February 20

At lunchtime on my way home, a shadow fell over me and I looked up and it was an owl! I've never seen an owl flying around during the day. It flew right over me and landed on a tree above me. It was still up there when I walked by. That was very strange. I have to remember to ask Grandma about it. Why would an owl do that?

Tuesday, February 21

I got another letter from Mother when we got home after school.

February 14, 1967
Dear Violet,

How are you today? I am sending you five dollars so that you can spend it on something you like. We are all doing all right here. Your brother and sister are fine and Izzy is doing okay too. We all went ice fishing last Saturday and Izzy got the biggest trout that I have ever seen! It was huge! People at the Band Office were taking pictures of it when Izzy stopped by there on the way home. I think he was just showing off, and we ended up giving half of it to the family next door because they happened to be there too. Since they saw the fish, we had to share it with them. Here I was thinking we could get more than three meals out of it. It serves me right for not thinking of sharing it in the first place.

I talked to Grandma yesterday. I called the store there to get a message to Grandma but she happened to be at the store and I got to talk to her right away. She doesn't like to use the phone herself to call me, because she has to crank the handle and talk to the dispatcher and then has to talk to someone else at the Band Office before she can talk to me, if I happen to be busy and not the first person to pick up the phone.

She said that you were probably feeling really sad about not being able to come home at Christmas, so I decided to write again and send you some money to buy your favourite chocolate or the toffee you like. Please cheer up and not feel too low. Find something that interests you. How are you doing on that Blackie book? Keep yourself busy. Work hard and remember that you will come home for the summer.

Write soon.

Your Mother,
Emily

Wednesday, February 22

snowing hard — *kichi-soogepoon*
very windy — *kichinoodin*
window — *wasachigun*
squirrel — *achitamoo*
beaver — *amik*
lynx — *pishiew*
porcupine — *kaag*

Thursday, February 23

I got a cotton kerchief for a dollar at Kresge's yesterday from the money Mother sent.

I was sitting on my bed just before supper and I began rolling the cloth into a frog, the way that Grandma showed me. That one was easy. I undid it and began rolling a rabbit, but I almost forgot how to roll the cloth so that the ears popped up. I was working on a partridge, to get the wings to come out properly, when one of the older girls walked by my bed. She immediately grabbed the cloth and whispered, "What is the matter with you!" and flattened out my kerchief and threw it at me. "What?" I said. She glared at me and whispered back, "It's from *home* — not allowed!!"

I really hate this place.

Friday, February 24

    wolverine — *kwingoaagae*
    wolf — *ma-ingan*
    rabbit — *wabooze*
    moose — *mooz*
    fisher — *ojiig*
    muskrat — *washushk*

Saturday, February 25

We were coming up the stairs after lunch and I saw Miss Scott at my locker. She had the door open and she had my papers in her hand. I almost had a heart attack! I saw that she had my Blackie story book where I keep my diaries inside. A shock went through me and I rushed forward and I smiled at her and said, "Oh, you've found my story! Here, let me show you the drawing I am doing that's going to be the cover." She smiled and handed me the papers and I pulled out my drawings and we laughed when I showed her my first attempts at the dog face. Then, she moved on to the next one.

Phew! That was too close! I am still shaking.

Sunday, February 26

I had better answer Mother's letter.

February 26, 1967

Dear Mother,

Thank you for your letter. I'm glad you guys had fun camping in the snow. That roasted meat over the fire would have tasted good. I can't wait to see Lyndon's doggie. You never said what his name is. Thank you for your second letter and the money. I bought a kerchief with it. It's beige with little pink flowers on it. It's really pretty.

I'm working hard at school and learning a lot about the English language. I am not saying *that I truly understand it yet, but I guess I will, in time.*

It has been very cold here with a lot of blowing snow.

We went to the Chapel for Sunday service this morning and I realized that I was singing along to the hymns. I must have learned them when I wasn't paying attention! I like us singing all together in the Chapel. I've never done that before.

I can't wait for the weather to get warmer. Spring will be here soon.

Write again soon.

> *Your daughter,*
> *Violet*

Tuesday, February 28

marten — *wabisheshi*

fox — *wagoosh*

mink — *shangueshi* (This is the same word for a quarter — 25¢. I wonder why this is the only coin that actually has a name. The others do not. I'll have to remember to ask Grandma. Maybe that was all a mink pelt was worth when the coins came along.)

skunk — *shigaag*

weasel — *shingoos*

134

Thursday, March 2

I am still struggling with "parts of speech." I still think the English language is a long, complicated mix of nouns, verbs, adjectives, blah, blah, blah! #!%*&@

I keep getting very frustrated, then I get angry. I can't take much more of this. I want to go home! I had another crying fit last night. I woke up from a nightmare. I dreamed that Grandma was calling, but there was so much bush that I could not find her. I was running around searching and calling and I kept hearing her calling me, but I could not find her!

I had a hard time going back to sleep.

I am also having trouble remembering the names of the types of snow in Anishinabe, since I have to write it down in English.

Snow is *koon*.

It is snowing is *sookpoon*.

Deep snow is *ishpagoonaga*.

I can't remember what sleet is called??? I've been thinking about that since last week.

I can't remember icicle either! Now, I just feel like crying!

I don't hear anyone even whispering the Anishinabe or Cree language, ever since the fall night of the girl saying the Lord's Prayer. I tried asking one of the girls to whisper the word for "icicle" to me but she just glared at me and walked away.

Friday, March 3

I've been practising writing with my left hand. I was born left-handed but the teachers at home used to hit my left hand with a ruler if they caught me writing with it. So I had to learn to write with my right hand. Since then, I have been writing with my right hand. So now I'm going to write with my left hand in my diary.

Saturday, March 4

I was really feeling sad last night and found that I was running my hand through my hair like Grandma used to do when I would sleep beside her as a little girl. She used to say "You're a good girl" over and over again until I fell asleep. I began to relax and it helped me go to sleep, imagining Grandma saying that over and over.

Sunday, March 5

I am getting pretty good writing with my left hand in just three days. It came back pretty fast.

Like learning to walk. I can't tell the difference between my left and right hand now. I hold the paper a bit crooked to keep my letters straight though.

Wednesday, March 8

    trout — *namegos*
    sturgeon — *nama*
    pickerel — *oganse*
    whitefish — *atikameg*
    sucker — *namebin*
    pike — *kinoozhe*

I got upset today at a white girl at school. She called me a name that I didn't really understand. I knew it was bad, but I did not react and just turned around and walked away. I find that when I stroke my hair from my forehead and run my hand through my hair and repeat "You're a good girl," over and over, it really helps. Then I go to sleep.

Friday, March 10

My Anishinabe conversation is still okay. It was just the names of things that I was starting to forget. I just keep talking to myself so I don't lose the words. I pretend that I am telling a story to Grandma.

I twisted my ankle on my way from school this afternoon. It is pretty swollen. I've been limping around all evening and will probably have to limp around all weekend too.

Saturday, March 11

My ankle is not too bad this morning.

I made a sketch of Grandma ice fishing. She's kneeling down on a bed of spruce boughs. Her ice chisel is sticking into the snow beside the water hole. There's the toboggan beside her and she's holding a stick with her fishing line tied to the end of it. As always, she has her kerchief over her head and her thick scarf around her neck. I drew her shadow beside her but I then had to make shadows of all the other objects around her. I thought I was all done, but then noticed that I had missed the shadow of the chisel.

I think she'll laugh when she sees the size of the trout that's lying on top of her toboggan.

Monday, March 13

There was an announcement on the intercom when we got home after school.

We are being sent home for Easter!

We are going home for Easter!!! Can't wait! Can't wait! Can't wait!!

Tuesday, March 14

I just had a horrible thought. What if they find this diary and then, as punishment, what if they don't let me go home? What if they find this before I can get away?

I wish there was somewhere safe where I can hide it, but there is nowhere!

Miss Tanner doesn't pay much attention to us younger girls. It's the oldest girls that she's always on about. She found a pack of cigarettes in someone's shoes yesterday. The girl was sent to the office. Don't know what happened to her, but when she came back into the dorm, she looked like she had been crying.

Friday, March 17

It is St. Patrick's Day today. I have no idea who St. Patrick is either. They say Saint, so he must have something to do with Church, like the man with the angels around him in the coloured windows at the Church. Maybe he is St. Patrick. But the angels look like little round naked boys

— like the Cupid on our Valentine's cards — that are flying around him. I have no idea. But then how would that have anything to do with the green clovers and green stringers they put up at the school? That makes no sense to me — at all!!

We had shepherd's pie for supper. Can't figure out why they call it a pie when it is just hamburger with peas and corn and topped with potatoes! It was good anyway.

I have nothing else to write about.

Monday, March 20

When we got here after school, the kids were hitting each other with snowballs. I was just about to run inside when the door opened. I glanced back and I saw Johnny with his eyes on me, so I ducked, and the snowball exploded right on Miss Tanner's face as she was coming out the door! Everyone froze. She wiped the snow off her face and pointed to Johnny and pointed to the main door. She never said a word, and Johnny walked in front of her, with his neck buried in his shoulders, to the main door where the Principal's office was. A few kids giggled when the door closed, but I ran inside and up the stairs to write this. That was quite funny actually!

Tuesday, March 21

Going home tomorrow!

All the girls are bustling around, all very nervous and anxious to get out of here!

We were given a pair of black pants and sweaters to wear home.

We are not allowed to take anything else with us.

Wednesday, March 22

After breakfast, we were given a sandwich bag for our lunch. I shoved my diary booklets and my Blackie story, along with a pencil tucked between the pages, inside the front of my pants, and pulled the sweater over them before we lined up to go downstairs to get our jackets and boots on.

I am on the train now and there are three of us girls. There are a lot of people coming and going along the aisle whenever the train stops.

We ate our sandwiches whenever we got hungry. I shoved my papers into the empty paper bag. It was around noon when we had to get off to change trains. I remembered this place. It was where we had to spend the night in September. It seems like ages ago, in another lifetime.

Finally, we are on the way home.

One of the girls got off the train just around supper hour. I remembered her the first time I saw her at the park, when she arrived with bright red fingernails! That was the last time I saw nail polish on her hands. She was one who stopped talking altogether. I used to call her Paris in my mind.

About an hour later we were getting very hungry.

It is quite dark now and there are soldiers on the train, making a lot of noise, and they're getting drunk. They are singing one song after another. I wish they would shut up!

I just recognized the train station we pulled out of. I will be home in about half an hour. That was the place that Grandma and I used to come for the rummage sale at the Church!

That young soldier is leaning over my seat again. I feel like punching him in the face!

I just look out at the moonlit hills, trees, lakes and rock cliffs. He has just left again after wanting to know what I was writing. Beast! I notice that I get very angry quickly now.

Thursday, March 23

I didn't get a chance to write anything when I got home. We were busy being so happy!

I woke up this morning and lay there with my eyes closed, waiting for the wake-up bell. Then I opened my eyes and saw the logs in front of my face. I was never so happy!!!

I am home!

Grandma is outside somewhere, and I just had to write down what a happy meeting it was when I got off the train and found Grandma standing there! We moved away from the group that was getting on the train and we just stood there holding on to each other. I thought I could actually hear her heart beating, we were hanging on to each other so close together! Then the train pulled away and soon there were just the two of us there. She seemed smaller and she told me that I was bigger and taller.

When the red tail lights of the train disappeared around the bend, we stepped onto the tracks. Grandma guided us along the railroad tracks with her flashlight. It was absolutely quiet, only our footsteps on the snow and our breathing, and we kept looking at each other and smiling. Soon we were off the tracks and onto the little trail to her cabin. The moon was bright and I could see the cabin and its shadow loom up in front of us as we came out of the bushes. It was so good to be home!

I was very hungry and she dished out a bowl of macaroni in tomato sauce with diced bologna in it. She buttered a chunk of bannock for me too. It was delicious!

She sat at the table beside the lamp and told me all the news that had happened since I left. Then she told me that she had sent me five dollars five times. *I never got it!* Only the one time! That really made me angry, because she must have had to go without something else to spare me the money.

I noticed the Valentine's card that I sent her tacked with a small nail on the window frame. She said it was really pretty. I asked about the letter and she said that there was no letter with it, just the card.

After a breakfast of porridge, Grandma wants to take me to the store and see what we would have for our lunch and supper. She liked my glasses. She laughed when I told her that I had no idea that there was something wrong with my eyes. Then she rummaged around in one of her pockets and stuck a pair of glasses on her nose. When she turned and looked at me, I almost choked when she blinked from huge buggy eyes through the lenses. I laughed so hard, I had tears in my eyes when she came and sat down and said that they were "reading glasses." She only puts them on when she reads.

That was funny! She is lying on her bed now, reading a book that the new teacher gave her.

Just before lunch, we set off to the store. As we came around the corner, I could see Blackie by his dog house. He stood up and slowly walked toward us. He gave a soft *woof* and then his tail started wagging and then he ran toward me and jumped up. He almost knocked me down and his sloppy tongue got me on the chin before I could push him down. I petted his head and he was very happy. His whole back end was just wiggling back and forth. Bill came out of his cabin with an axe in his hand and he turned and saw us. He said, "You're back. Someone's happy to see you." I smiled and said hello. He was on his way to split some wood beside his cabin and he called Blackie and he watched us go by.

There were quite a few people at the store. Everyone wanted to take a good look at me, saying to Grandma that I had grown up. That was embarrassing. Grandma bought some salt pork and dry beans, a chunk of bologna and some flour. When we got home, we had fried bologna sandwiches made with some leftover bologna from yesterday.

We are going ice fishing this afternoon.

Friday, March 24

It is Good Friday today. I don't much care why it is called Good Friday. Something to do about Jesus, maybe.

We just had breakfast of porridge and we are sitting around the table. Grandma is making something from moose leather and doing bead-work. I decided to write this note in my diary. I didn't get a chance to write anything when we got back from ice fishing yesterday. It was slushy so we couldn't sit down on the ice. So we had to lean over the ice holes. We managed to get only one jack fish. She fried that and served it with some rice. We were hungry and it was wonderful!

It's softly snowing outside. We have enough wood stacked by the door so we don't need to cut more for a few days anyway. It's nice and warm in here and the teapot is on the stove, keeping warm.

Grandma said that a Minister was supposed to arrive to have a Good Friday service at the Church, but he got sick. He usually makes his rounds to the small communities along the rail-road tracks during special religious holidays.

I feel very peaceful now and the tight ache across my chest that I always had at Residential School is gone.

Saturday, March 25

Grandma was looking over my diaries, placing them in order of dates. She said she would read them when she was alone. I didn't ask her why. Maybe she didn't want me to remember what I was feeling at the time I wrote them.

I asked her whatever became of her own dia-ries when she was a young girl. She said that she had kept them in a box and one day when she was alone after they had sent Mother off to Residential School, her cabin had burnt down and she lost everything that she had, except for a shed at the back that managed to escape the fire. She was alone in the bush at the time. She found some clothes in the shed and she dressed in layers and made her way back here to the village.

There was an abandoned cabin at the other

end of the community that she was able to fix up and made liveable. People gave her what they could of things that she could use.

That summer, just before Mother came home from Residential School, the men of the community all came together and built her this cabin that she still lives in.

Sunday, March 26

We went ice fishing again today. It is getting very slushy, worse than on Thursday, but we got four trout. We had a lot of fun. Now Grandma is cooking potatoes in the pot with the trout. She also has canned peas in the small pot heating by the stove. There are no fresh vegetables at the store in the winter time. Just potatoes and carrots.

I know how to clean the fish, I just don't know how they made the things I ate at the Residential School. I bet I would be able to find a cookbook in Sandy Bay. It actually has a library there.

This is really funny! I just noticed that there is a message on the back package of the flour Grandma bought from the store. I turned it over and it said that if you want a recipe book, you just have to write to them with your address and they will send you one!

I showed it to Grandma and she gave me an envelope and a sheet of paper. I'll send in my mailing address to the flour company. Grandma was laughing at me.

Monday, March 27

We had fried rabbit with rice for supper. It was very delicious.

I got into the habit of writing down what I had for supper at Residential School.

I had also got into the habit of feeling very angry all the time while I was at Residential School too. Now I do not feel that at all. It is like it has all been washed away. This is the longest I have gone without feeling angry.

Easter Monday today. I would have totally forgotten about Easter, but a special Minister got off the train this morning. He is the Bishop, they say. Grandma and I went to the Church when the bell rang. I was curious. After the service, the Bishop stood at the door and shook hands with everyone. He was telling some older girls and their parents to stay and they stood just inside the Church. When it was my turn, he also pulled me aside and asked us to wait with the other girls and their parents. There were no boys our age there.

When everyone was gone, the Bishop explained to us about Confirmation. Since us girls had not been confirmed yet, he asked us to stay. He had a couple of hours before the train came, when he would get back on again. When the Confirmation was explained, the parents and the girls gathered outside and they all nodded and Grandma asked me if I wanted to be confirmed, I said no. So, Grandma turned around and I followed her home. There were five girls that stayed.

Tuesday, March 28

I am supposed to go back to Residential School tomorrow.

Grandma just asked me if I wanted to go back and I said no.

Wednesday, March 29

Grandma just went to the store to call my mother. She says I can't stay here because I would be sent back to the Residential School anyway, since the Indian Affairs guys know where I am. If Mother comes to get me, I could go to school at the Reserve for the rest of the year. I guess that's better than going back to the Residential School.

I got on the Residential School list because I

got to Grade 5 at Flint Lake Indian Day School. I could just join the rest of the Grade 5 students on the Reserve for now, even though we will be sent somewhere for higher grades anyway, after we finish Grade 5.

Friday, March 31

We had boiled partridge with dumplings for supper and it was very delicious.

Mother is going to come and get me sometime next week.

I guess I could hide out in the bush somewhere if someone shows up to take me back to the Residential School. They'd have nowhere to stay until the next train comes in anyway. Grandma and I would just have to go somewhere for the day.

Emma is not here because she already came home at Christmas and she won't be home until school is over in June.

Monday, April 3

Mother just arrived on the train this afternoon. I ran to the train tracks when I heard the train come in. Grandma was busy making lunch. When the train went by, I waited to see Mother come along the tracks after the rest of the people moved off, and then I saw her. I ran to meet her and she dropped her suitcase when I gave her a big hug. It was so good to see her! We are getting on the train tomorrow to head off to the Reserve. She works, so she can't get much time off. I'm going to miss Grandma when we leave.

Rob came to the cabin asking if Grandma had any suggestions about their sick baby. The baby girl has a bad cold and has trouble breathing. He thought he'd come and ask Grandma first before his wife had to take the baby to the hospital, which is over three hours away by train. Grandma rummaged around in her "healing box" as I call it, before she wrapped a bundle of herbs and went off with him.

Mother and I just finished playing cards and she's gone to take a nap on my bed. Grandma is not back yet.

After supper

Grandma said she made a steam tent with herbs for the baby to breathe, and then a cedar poultice for the baby's chest. She thinks the little girl will be all right in a few days.

I hate to leave Grandma. I would much rather

stay here, but I know that I have to go back to the Reserve.

Tuesday, April 4

Mother slept on my bed beside me last night. I'm so used to sleeping by myself that I had a very hard time going to sleep. We're just sitting around at the table drinking tea. It's another hour yet before the train comes.

Saturday, April 8

We're at the Reserve now. Mother talked to the teacher and he's going to allow me to join the Senior classes on Monday.

We had fried pickerel and canned spaghetti for supper. Eliza was really excited when I got here. Lyndon just looked at me and shrugged.

Lyndon's dog is really cute! No wonder Mother couldn't tell me his name because it is "Maangoons" — Little Loon — because he has a black head, and the black hair stops around his neck and the rest of him is spotted in white. He *does* look like a loon! All he wants to do is play.

I have to share a room with Eliza but that's okay. She has her own little bed in one corner and I have a single bed in the other. There's a window on my side and I can feel the wind from the window. There is only a plastic sheet covering it. There's old linoleum on the floor and it gets very cold. I have to wear thick socks all the time. I don't know how I forgot my moccasins at Grandma's. She had made a pair for me when I was at Residential School. She said that she meant to give them to me at Christmas.

Too bad I couldn't stay with Grandma.

Sunday, April 9

Grandma called and left a message at the store saying that she would call again at a certain time, so Mother and I went to the store at that time, and sure enough, the phone rang and the storekeeper handed us the phone. A package had arrived for me! Mother laughed when I told her what it probably is. My cookbook! We just had to go to Grandma's to get it! It was an excuse to see Grandma again.

Monday, April 10

Mother fixed my bed again yesterday morning, before we headed off to her work at the Band Office and me to school.

I usually just straighten out my bed in the

mornings at Grandma's. Here, there is a cotton sheet around the mattress and a quilted blanket on top. But Mother had always insisted that I fold my blankets under the mattress whenever I was here, and I never asked why. Now I recognize that she is still trying to do what she was trained to do at Residential School. So I deliberately left my blankets hanging down. When I came back from school today, they were tucked in under the mattress. Mother had remade my bed while I was at school. I ripped the blanket off and left it hanging down again.

She didn't say anything.

Tuesday, April 11

Mother did not remake my bed again. It was as I had left it this morning.

We had macaroni mixed with canned tomato soup with square chunks of canned Klik mixed in. I made a face at Izzy when Mother's back was turned, and he grinned and winked at me. I really think I am going to have to learn to cook. I can't wait to get my hands on that cookbook! I didn't get a chance to go to the library when we passed through Sandy Bay on the way to the airplane base.

Wednesday, April 12

There was a gang of girls here that used to make my life miserable. They'd catch me coming or going from school. They never touched me, they just made up songs and teased me about Izzy not being my father and asked where my own father was and what his name is. The leader was a big girl with a huge nose. Big Nose has apparently married a boy from another Reserve, so she had to move there, so now there is no gang of girls. I am very happy about that.

Sunday, April 16

We are back at Flint Lake.

Mother and I got here yesterday. It is so nice to visit Grandma! I finally had time to visit Rob and his wife and baby. I arrived with my first attempt at making a pot of chili. It tasted really good, I thought, but I was not sure if it tasted too spicy for them. After a taste, they said that it was very, very good! His wife's name is Sarah and the baby is Matilda. She is also expecting another baby.

I spent my time telling them about the Residential School and about the daily activities. They were full of questions, as they too had gone to Residential Schools, and also their siblings.

I was very surprised to hear that Emma was home. I asked Grandma why she came back, and she said that she heard Emma had been really sick in the city, but that is all she knew. I thought that I could go visit her, but we have to catch the evening train and then sleep overnight at a hotel in the next town before catching the plane back to the Reserve.

Izzy wasn't too happy, as this was a rather expensive trip just to visit and get my cookbook. I wanted to see Grandma really bad too, and this time remembered to pack my moccasins.

Mother and Grandma laughed when I was thumbing through all the recipes that I was going to cook.

Sunday, April 23

After Church today, people came up to say hello and some welcomed me back home. It doesn't feel like home though. I'd rather be back home at Flint Lake with Grandma. I asked Izzy on the way home why everyone was so friendly to me all of a sudden. He winked and said that now that I was a young woman, every parent was looking me over as a potential daughter-in-law. My mouth fell open and I think I had better leave as soon as I can!

Monday, April 24

I don't feel like writing like this every day now. It feels like there is no purpose anymore. At Residential School, I was basically writing to Grandma, and now there is no need.

So far, I have baked some cookies, raisin pie (my pie crust was a bit hard), made meatballs, French toast, brown beans, shepherd's pie (had to use hamburger — recipe says beef chunks), spaghetti with meat sauce, casseroles (I had to put in other stuff for some stuff they don't have at the store). I haven't tried bread or cakes yet.

Later

Mother and I went to the store after school and I noticed that some of the food packages have recipes at the back or under the labels too. The storekeeper noticed me looking at the boxes and cans and writing down the recipes in my notebook. Then he asked me if I'd like to work there after school and on weekends to clean up spills, sweep the floor and dust the place. He does have a caretaker, but the guy just mostly keeps the meat and dairy section clean and mops the floor.

He asked Mother and she said sure and how much would he pay me. She was really happy when he said how much he'd pay. That was one thing I learned at Residential School — how to clean things properly. I have my first paying job!

Sunday, June 4

I go to Church every Sunday now. Most times by myself, since Mother and Izzy are usually busy getting fish or hunting for meat. I can also sing to my heart's content here. There are only a few old ladies who sing from the Cree syllabic hymn books, although they speak the Anishinabe language. They still do not have Anishinabe-language hymn books. We don't care — there are some young girls who sing from the English hymn books with me, and the old ladies join us in Anishinabe. It sounds really funny — the words are different but the music is still the same. We have a great time. The Minister lives on the Reserve and he is old with white hair, but he's nice. He just nods and smiles. I'm not sure he makes any more sense to me than the Minister down south.

Monday, June 5

I just found out that me and six other kids are going to be sent to a city in the south to go to high school there in the fall. There was a meeting at the school gym and we were told that we would be staying with white people in their own homes in the city. It would be just like the place Emma lived in while she went to high school, I guess.

I don't really know what it will feel like to live in white people's homes. Based on what I experienced with the white kids at King George School, I don't know about that. But I really have no choice and no say as to where I am being sent or where I will stay. They will just get us on a plane, then onto a train and then into a city to be dropped off at white people's homes, where we will stay while we go to a city school. I'm really not happy about all this, but I notice the other kids are all excited about going into the city! Idiots!!!

Mother says Izzy is getting fat and she's blaming it on my cooking! I got the storekeeper's wife to show me how to make bread, but I haven't tried it yet. I am kind of scared to try because I might end up with a big blob of dough!

Monday, July 3

We are back at Flint Lake and I am staying with Grandma for the summer!

Izzy bought a brand-new shining aluminum canoe for Grandma at the next town. They loaded it in the baggage car and Grandma had tears in her eyes when she realized it was for her when they were getting it off the train. Mother had bought a second-hand canvas tent from someone at the Reserve. After work on my last day, I asked the storekeeper how much the fishnet was in the corner. I told him that I would like to take it to my grandmother and he just pulled it out and handed it to me, saying that it had been taking up space in the store for a long time anyway. I couldn't believe it! I got it free for Grandma! I am looking forward to camping and fishing with Grandma all summer. For now, the tent is set up outside Grandma's cabin where Izzy, Mother, Lyndon and Eliza have moved in to stay for the week.

This is my last entry. I left my last sewn-seamed pages on top of Grandma's pillow.

Epilogue

That fall of 1967, Violet began her trip from the Reserve to the city with two other students. She had some money in her pocket. She also had a solid green suitcase that Izzy had bought for her. This time, there would be no one to take it away from her. Everything she had packed would be hers.

She boarded an airplane at the Reserve with two boys about her own age. They landed at the nearest town, stayed at a hotel that night, and very early the next morning, they walked to the train station across the street.

When they got to the train station, Violet found three girls sitting on one of the benches. The three had no luggage. They had slept on the benches in the station waiting room all night, not knowing where they were supposed to go. The girls had been told to get on the train by the storekeeper, who had the only phone in their community, but they were not told where to go once they reached the station. There was nothing open yet where they could have bought something to eat.

The ticket agent told them all at sunrise that the train pulling in was theirs. They got on the train and settled in for a long ride, as it would be stopping to deliver supplies and pick up freight all along the line to the city.

Around lunchtime, the six were very hungry, but there was nothing to eat on the train. They watched the small communities go by, one after the other — lakes, rocks and more lakes, surrounded by the many beautiful fall colours.

The four girls sat together. The two boys, in the opposite row of seats, seemed to be enjoying themselves.

Later in the afternoon, Violet realized that none of the girls had much to say. They answered her when she spoke to them, but otherwise they just looked out the window. She asked their names and soon discovered that none had ever left home before. They were scared, not knowing what to expect and what it would be like where they were going.

For the first time, Violet realized that she had more experience than any of them, and had a better idea of what life would be like in the city. So she told them what she thought it would be like to live in white families' homes and what the inside of the house would be like, based on her baby-sitting experience while she was at Residential School. That was the only white person's home she had ever entered. She also explained what the city high school might be like, and the bus they might have to take to go to school.

Violet listened to the girls telling each other about their lives and the loved ones they had left behind. When they tried to draw her in on their conversation, she found that she couldn't think of a thing to add, other than what she had already told them. She realized then that she didn't know how to talk to other girls her age. She had never had any friends her own age. She had no trouble, however, in telling them what they must do and what they should watch out for in the city.

At the first home Violet stayed, there were three other Anishinabe girls. Violet soon discovered the house rules. The girls were not allowed to sit outside, because the homeowners' neighbours might see them. They were not allowed into the living room to watch television. After school, they were to stay in their room and do their homework. Then they were called to supper, where they ate in silence. Their offer to wash the dishes was turned down. They were told not to touch anything, and to go back into their bed-room and get ready for the next school day.

As promised, Violet began her diary for Grandma on the first day of school, this time in a new shiny red diary that Grandma had given her. This one had a tiny gold lock. Never trusting anyone, Violet kept it locked in her suitcase at all times and took it out only when she wrote in it just before bed every evening.

The high school was large. In her homeroom, Violet found that there were eight Anishinabe students in a class of thirty. At lunchtime, she met twenty-five Anishinabe students and they all sat together in the cafeteria.

One day, as she was boarding the bus for home, Violet noticed two boys from the school who always hung around together. They got on the same bus as she did and sat down across the aisle from her. The older boy leaned over, saying that they were going downtown before heading home. He asked where she lived. She told him the street name, but then they couldn't talk anymore as other people got on.

When they reached downtown, Violet waited for the bus she would need to transfer to. The boys hung around with her, talking, until her bus came. They were brothers named Steve and Dave. Steve was older and the talkative one. After that day, they took to riding downtown with Violet to see her onto her next bus.

Toward the end of September, an announcement came on the school intercom that all Anishinabe students were to report to a particular room and wait there. Seven students from her class made their way down the hall with Violet, to find another group of students already standing there.

Violet asked one of the boys what this was about. He looked at her and told her firmly, "You are *not* to answer true. Just give any answer at all, but not the truth. Pretend you don't understand and pretend you don't know! We all do it."

Violet was puzzled. One by one, the students were called in. When it was her turn, Violet sat down where she was told. A man sat there with forms in front of him and a pen held poised. He began showing her weird squiggly lines on a page, then asked her what it was. On and on he went, from one page to another. Violet began to enjoy giving opposite answers to what she thought the lines might be, or just making answers up as she went along. Finally, she was told she could go. When she came out, she asked another girl,

"What was *that* all about?" The girl smiled. "The intelligence test," she said.

The girls Violet lived with stayed for about two weeks at their first home before they had to move again. It would be the first move of many.

As Christmastime neared and it was almost time to go home, Violet began having anxiety attacks and could not sleep. She was beginning to dread that something was going to happen to prevent her from getting home to Grandma again. Her mother and Izzy had agreed that she was to go to Flint Lake for Christmas, and they would see if they could visit her there at Grandma's. The Indian Affairs Student Counsellor agreed to the arrangement because it was simpler travel for Violet than going to her mother's Reserve.

But Violet did get to go home this time. After a long bus ride through a rough bush road, Violet's bus arrived at a town. She and three others got on a train from there. When the train stopped at Flint Lake, Grandma was there to meet Violet.

A huge storm prevented Violet's mother and family from coming to see her at Grandma's. After a joyous reunion with Grandma and a week spent chopping wood and ice fishing, Violet was back at the city high school. She kept writing in her journal, waiting until she could get back to Grandma. In all, she moved five times to different homes with her green suitcase that first year.

Violet stayed with her grandmother at Flint Lake every summer holiday for the next four years. In February of Violet's final year of high school, her grandmother died, alone in her cabin. Violet was devastated and took a long time to recover from her grief. Her grades began to slip. Finally, after struggling for weeks to catch up with her school work, she managed to pass her year and leave school behind. She never saw Steve and Dave again.

Violet never returned to Flint Lake. After her high-school graduation, she began work as a clerk at the Hudson's Bay store on the Reserve where her mother lived. Izzy had managed to build an extension to the home so that Violet could have her own bedroom.

When she turned twenty, Violet married the Grade 3 teacher who lived on the Reserve. They had four children. With them lived an all-black dog named Blackie.

To this day, the children of the northern First Nations must live in cities and towns, usually far from home and family, to attend high school.

Historical Note

This complicated part of Canada's history cannot be fully explored in the following paragraphs, and the existing research includes some variation in dates and numbers from different sources. But the sending away of Indigenous children from their families, often for years at a time, is so important we must make the attempt.

In the years between the early 1800s and mid-1980s, many children from as young as four years old were taken from their homes and sent to residential schools across Canada that were run by various church organizations and the federal government. The last federal residential school closed in 1984; the last residential school closed in 1998.

Changes to the Indian Act in 1894–1895 and in 1920 included compulsory education for Indigenous children, with the purpose of assimilation. This allowed the government to forcibly remove children from their parents and usher them into bush planes, trains and vehicles. Many parents were threatened with imprisonment or having their children permanently taken away if they protested.

For the most part, the children were to be taught how to integrate into the general society and therefore had to be taught and trained in skills, religious studies, domestic work, farm labour and various trades. Some authors have called the practices of households, farms, businesses and industries using these children as labourers, under the guise of training, "child and youth slavery." The students' mornings were normally reserved for book learning and religious instruction, and the afternoons given to domestic work, farm labour and trades.

In earlier years of the residential school program, the students usually lived and went to school in the same location: the residential schools. In later years, in the 1960s, the students living at residential schools were integrated into city and town public schools, taking their classes with the general population of students, as is the case in this story.

It is estimated that over 150,000 children attended the 139 residential schools across the country. What took place within these institutions is a disgrace in Canadian history. The children were psychologically, physically, emotionally and even sexually abused, and many died from contagious diseases or while trying to get home. At some residential schools, the children were poorly clothed and inadequately fed, and suffered from malnutrition. The report of the Truth and Reconciliation Commission states that at least three thousand children died in these schools. Chair for the Commission, Chief Justice Murray Sinclair, has said that, "seven generations of aboriginal children were denied their identity through a systematic and concerted effort to extinguish their culture, language and spirit."

At sixteen years of age, the children were sent home. They found themselves in communities that they knew nothing about. Those who stayed in residential school for years at a time had to have name tags pinned to their jackets so that their parents would know who they were — the children were so young when they were taken, their parents could no longer recognize them.

The children who grew up in these residential schools had no knowledge of family, love or community. They had also lost their language and culture and been stripped of all identity. Many never recovered, and suffered all their lives — in many cases, with horrible social problems, often ending in suicide. Those who tried to reintegrate into the community married and had children, but knew nothing of raising children or meeting the needs of a child, since they had never experienced such things in their lives. The cycle of damaged child-rearing practices has continued for generations. Some literature describes this part of Canadian history as cultural genocide.

In the 1990s, many of the victims of the residential schools sued the churches and the Canadian government. The Royal Commission on Aboriginal Peoples was created in 1991, followed by the Aboriginal Healing Foundation in 1998. In 2006, the Indian Residential School Settlement Agreement was signed, a $1.9-billion settlement that prompted an apology from Prime Minster Stephen Harper, on behalf of all Canadians, on June 11, 2008. The Truth and Reconciliation Commission was launched by the federal government in 2009.

For their involvement in the residential schools, churches began presenting their apologies. The Oblates of Mary Immaculate issued a formal apology in 1991; the Anglican Church in 1993. The apology from the Presbyterian Church came in 1994. In 1998, the United Church also offered an apology. The Catholic Church, which was responsible for about seventy-five percent of the residential schools, also presented its apology through the Pope in 2009.

The report of the Truth and Reconciliation Commission, before which thousands of Indigenous people had testified about their experiences and the effects they still lived with, was published in late 2015. All the materials, statements and documents that have been collected are now housed at the National Centre for Truth and Reconciliation located at the University of Manitoba, in Chancellor's Hall.

It is estimated that about 150,000 Indigenous children were removed from their communities and forced to attend residential schools, from the early 1800s until the late 1900s. Children were made to wear uniform clothing unlike what many would have worn at home.

When students attended class, the girls were often separated from the boys.

Sameness of clothing and even of haircuts was the norm. Upon reaching the schools, students were given a number, which would be attached to their clothing.

The dormitories were often sparse and uniform. The children could seldom interact with siblings who were at the school at the same time, and prayer time was regimented.

Girls usually had their meals separately from the boys.

Washroom facilities were often very different from what the children would be used to at home.

Girls were often given instruction in cooking or sewing, and some helped to prepare meals.

A residential school survivor holds his granddaughter at a Truth and Reconciliation Commission audience.

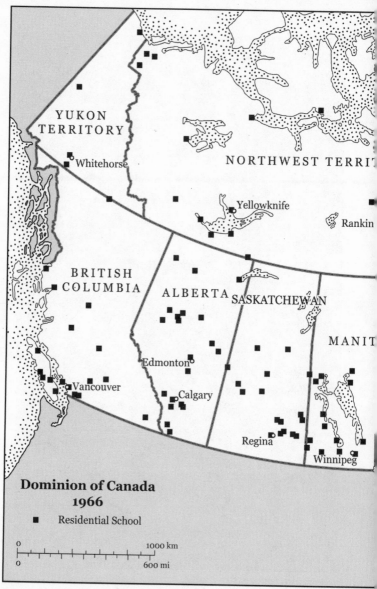

Dominion of Canada
1966

■ Residential School

0   1000 km

0   600 mi

Approximately 150,000 First Nations, Métis and Inuit children were sent awa
residential schools all across Canada between the early 1800s and the late 19

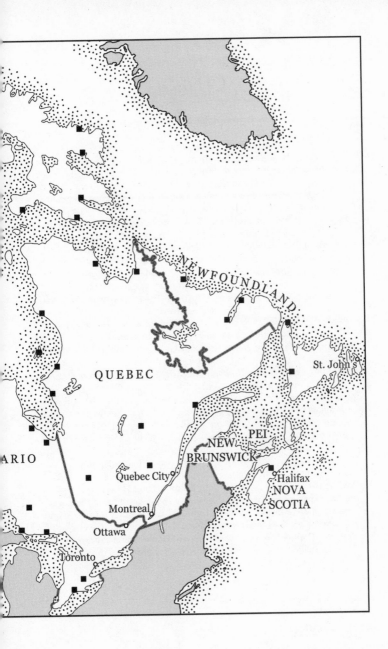

NEWFOUNDLAND

QUEBEC

St. John's

PEI

NEW
BRUNSWICK

ARIO

Quebec City

Halifax

NOVA
SCOTIA

Montreal

Ottawa

Toronto

Credits

Cover cameo: Courtesy of Ruby Slipperjack.
Cover background (detail): *St. Paul's Residential School, Blood Reserve, Alberta*; Atterson Studio, Cardston, Alberta; Glenbow Archives NC-7-859.
Page 174: *Girls at residential school, Ile-a-la-Crosse, northern Saskatchewan*; Thomas Waterworth; Glenbow Archives PD-353-22.
Page 175: *R.C. Indian Residential School Study Time, [Fort] Resolution, N.W.T.*; Library and Archives Canada / PA-042133.
Page 176: *R.C. Brandon Indian Residential School, students at their desks in a classroom, 1946*; National Film Board of Canada, Photothèque collection / Library and Archives Canada / PA-048571.
Page 177: *Prayer time in the girls' dormitory at Cecilia Jeffrey Indian Residential School near Kenora, c. 1950–53*; The Presbyterian Church in Canada Archives.
Page 178: *Mealtime at First Nations residential school, Norway House, Manitoba*; Glenbow Archives NA-3239-6.
Page 179: *The Cree Residential School at La Tuque, Québec*; University of Connecticut.
Page 180: *Cooking class, Indian Residential School, Edmonton*; United Church of Canada Archives, UCCA, 93.049P/885N.
Page 181: *Former Northwest Territories premier Stephen Kakfwi, a residential school survivor, holds his granddaughter Sadeya Kakfwi-Scott while standing with the audience at the Truth and Reconciliation Commission in Ottawa on Tuesday, June 2, 2015*; Adrian Wyld / THE CANADIAN PRESS
Pages 182–183: Map by Paul Heersink, Paperglyphs.
The publisher wishes to thank Anishinaabemowin elder Shirley Ida Williams-nee Pheasant, Indigenous Studies, Trent University, for sharing her expertise on this topic. She says: "The greatest thing the government can do as penance is to restore the language they destroyed and restore the pride in the culture of First Nations through the education system." Thanks also to Barbara Hehner for her careful checking of the factual details, and to Paul Heersink for providing the map.

About the Author

Ruby Slipperjack is a member of the Eabametoong First Nation and she is fluent in her Anishinabe language. She was born and raised at her father's trapline at Whitewater Lake, Ontario, and entered a one-room Indian Day School, with no knowledge of English, at the age of seven. These schools were built all along the Canadian National Railway line where there were enough school-aged children to attend. After Grade 5 she was sent to Residential School, and later attended a city school. For that period, she lived in a room-and-board situation with non-native families until she graduated from high school. She retained her traditional knowledge and still practises her Nation's cultural activities at her family's homeland at Whitewater Lake.

Ruby completed her formal education with a B.A. in History, B.Ed. and M.Ed. from Lakehead University and a Ph.D. in Educational Studies from the University of Western Ontario. She is a tenured, full professor in the Indigenous Learning Department at Lakehead University. Her prior novels include *Honour the Sun, Silent Words, Weesquachak and the Lost Ones, Little Voice, Weesquachak* and *Dog Tracks*. She contributed stories to the Dear Canada anthologies *Hoping for Home: Stories of Arrival* and *A Time for Giving: Ten Tales of Christmas*.

While the events described and some of the characters in this book
may be based on actual historical events,
Violet Pesheens is a fictional character created by the author,
and her diary is a work of fiction.

Library and Archives Canada Cataloguing in Publication

Slipperjack, Ruby, 1952-, author
These are my words : the residential school diary of Violet
Pesheens / Ruby Slipperjack.

ISBN 978-1-4431-3318-0 (hardback).--ISBN 978-1-4431-3319-7 (html)

1. Native girls--Canada--Juvenile fiction. 2. Native peoples--
Canada--Residential schools--Juvenile fiction. I. Title.
PS8587.L53T54 2016   jC813'.54   C2016-900404-X
                                               C2016-900405-8

6 5 4 3 2 1   Printed in Canada 114   16 17 18 19 20

First printing September 2016

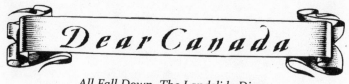

Dear Canada

*All Fall Down, The Landslide Diary
of Abby Roberts* by Jean Little

Alone in an Untamed Land, The Filles du Roi *Diary
of Hélène St. Onge* by Maxine Trottier

*Banished from Our Home, The Acadian Diary
of Angélique Richard* by Sharon Stewart

*Blood Upon Our Land, The North West Resistance Diary
of Josephine Bouvier* by Maxine Trottier

*Brothers Far from Home, The World War I Diary
of Eliza Bates* by Jean Little

A Christmas to Remember, Tales of Comfort and Joy

*A Country of Our Own, The Confederation Diary
of Rosie Dunn* by Karleen Bradford

*Days of Toil and Tears, The Child Labour Diary
of Flora Rutherford* by Sarah Ellis

*The Death of My Country, The Plains of Abraham Diary
of Geneviève Aubuchon* by Maxine Trottier

*A Desperate Road to Freedom, The Underground Railroad
Diary of Julia May Jackson* by Karleen Bradford

*Exiles from the War, The War Guests Diary
of Charlotte Mary Twiss* by Jean Little

*Flame and Ashes, The Great Fire Diary
of Triffie Winsor,* by Janet McNaughton

Footsteps in the Snow, The Red River Diary
of Isobel Scott by Carol Matas

Hoping for Home, Stories of Arrival

If I Die Before I Wake, The Flu Epidemic Diary
of Fiona Macgregor by Jean Little

No Safe Harbour, The Halifax Explosion Diary
of Charlotte Blackburn by Julie Lawson

Not a Nickel to Spare, The Great Depression Diary
of Sally Cohen by Perry Nodelman

An Ocean Apart, The Gold Mountain Diary
of Chin Mei-ling by Gillian Chan

Orphan at My Door, The Home Child Diary
of Victoria Cope by Jean Little

Pieces of the Past, The Holocaust Diary
of Rose Rabinowitz by Carol Matas

A Prairie as Wide as the Sea, The Immigrant Diary
of Ivy Weatherall by Sarah Ellis

Prisoners in the Promised Land, The Ukrainian Internment
Diary of Anya Soloniuk by Marsha Forchuk Skrypuch

A Rebel's Daughter, The 1837 Rebellion Diary
of Arabella Stevenson by Janet Lunn

A Ribbon of Shining Steel, The Railway Diary
of Kate Cameron by Julie Lawson

A Sea of Sorrows, The Typhus Epidemic Diary
of Johanna Leary by Norah McClintock

A Season for Miracles, Twelve Tales of Christmas

That Fatal Night, The Titanic *Diary
of Dorothy Wilton* by Sarah Ellis

*A Time for Giving,
Ten Tales of Christmas*

*Torn Apart, The Internment Diary
of Mary Kobayashi by* Susan Aihoshi

*To Stand On My Own, The Polio Epidemic Diary
of Noreen Robertson* by Barbara Haworth-Attard

*A Trail of Broken Dreams, The Gold Rush Diary
of Harriet Palmer* by Barbara Haworth-Attard

*Turned Away, The World War II Diary
of Devorah Bernstein* by Carol Matas

*Where the River Takes Me, The Hudson's Bay Company
Diary of Jenna Sinclair* by Julie Lawson

*Whispers of War, The War of 1812 Diary
of Susannah Merritt* by Kit Pearson

*Winter of Peril, The Newfoundland Diary
of Sophie Loveridge* by Jan Andrews

*With Nothing But Our Courage, The Loyalist Diary
of Mary MacDonald* by Karleen Bradford

Go to www.scholastic.ca/dearcanada for information on
the Dear Canada series — see inside the books, read an
excerpt or a review, post a review, and more.